A   h

A Novel

Jill Ammon-Wexler

CLEAR VISION PRESS
CAPITOLA, CALIFORNIA

A MOMENT OF TRUTH: A NOVEL
Copyright © 1998 Jill Ammon-Wexler

For information contact the publisher.

Published in the United States of America by:
Clear Vision Press
Post Office Box 608
Capitola, California 95010 USA
E-mail: Clearvis@cruzio.com

ISBN: 0-9657459-0-2
LC: 97-091696

Printed in the United States of America
Publication Date: August 1998

10 9 8 7 6 5 4 3 2 1

Previously released as:
A Moment of Truth: A Transformational Novel

ℭℬℰↃ

AN AUTHOR'S NOTE

IF WE READ the signs correctly, *something* is afoot today on Earth. Something the most serious thinkers of our day are calling a paradigm shift. Something our scientists and ecologists are calling a global ecological crisis. Something our medicine men and shamans claim was predicted many centuries ago by great seers such as Nostradamus.

We each face our own dragons in today's deeply challenged times. Dare we ask ourselves: If I love the Earth enough, will it endure? Will there still be trees when I'm 80 or 90? Will my children be able to breath the air? Do I dare indulge in the luxury of such hope? Can I make a difference?

Our challenge is to discover the power to become warriors and manifest our dreams as reality. The seers are telling us – the time is now.

In my heart I believe that we can empower ourselves to live with passionate truth and meaning. That we can rise up like the Phoenix from out of the ashes of Earth's Great Change to create something bold and beautiful and new.

Since you were attracted to this book, you obviously share a similar vision. And so, dear reader, I respectfully dedicate this book to YOU and to your personal desire for empowerment and meaning. *May you stand tall in your Moment of Truth!*

℀℁

CHAPTER ONE

Higher reality has a way of breaking out unexpectedly…
moments when the all-knowing nucleus of the self
defeats the mind's narrow prejudices.

—*Deepak Chopra, MD*

THE MORNING HAD just begun to backlight the thick blanket of caustic, mustard-colored smog when the nightmare ripped into her already fitful sleep.

Diana gasped as everything solid dropped from beneath her. A searing light smashed against her eyelids, blinded her as a savage vortex of energy ripped her from the safety of her bed and spit her out into a swirling emptiness.

Her gut wrenched with each turn of the vortex.

Then, for the third time that night, everything was suddenly quiet. Too quiet.

She jammed herself down into a tight knot, but already knew it was too late. She felt, then saw the sickening green light racing at her again.

She braced herself, but the impact of the light tore her free from the grip of the vortex, then hurled her toward a massive, featureless wall.

A piercing cry exploded from her lungs as she smashed into the wall, a crumpled heap of torn flesh and shattered bones.

Hopeless fear clutched at her throat.

Her heart thundered against mangled ribs.

She tore wildly at the sheets in a desperate attempt to escape the nightmare. She tried to scream, no sound came; tried to run, but her shattered legs wouldn't support her.

She held her breath and desperately extended her senses out into the foul, thick yellow curtain of sulfurous gas that had risen around her broken body.

Then she heard it. The steady breathing of something large, very large. A tortured moan rasped out of the deepest, oldest part of herself as she made out the hulking outline through the mist.

The unblinking, searing red eyes stripped the last faint illusion of hope from her.

A terrible silence, then the air was shattered by a single victorious roar.

Her stomach convulsed as a fire ball burst from the dragon's mouth and engulfed her in flames.

"No." The scream tore from her lungs, freeing her from the grip of the nightmare just as the intense flames began to burn the flesh from her bones.

Diana lunged out of bed, dug her toes into the thick zebra striped rug, and swayed wildly for balance. "Cripes." She collapsed back onto the bed. "I can't take much more of this. Really can't." She ran her fingers through the sweat-drenched hair on the back of her neck, felt for the hard knots in the muscles. *Still there, tighter even than last night.*

She forced herself onto her feet, pressed her fingers into the cable-tight neck muscles, and shuffled unsteadily to the bedroom window. She pulled aside the French lace curtain and peered out at the smudgy, burnt orange morning sky.

"Ugh. Another Class 4 smog alert." Her tongue felt thick and somehow unfamiliar in her mouth. She sighed and jerked the curtain back across the window.

She jammed her arms into a crumpled cobalt blue satin dressing gown, sighed yet another ragged breath, and headed toward the bathroom.

Diana flipped on the bank of theater lights and peered reluctantly into the light-flooded mirror. The 40ish woman that stared back had gaunt cheeks, puffy eyes from lack of sleep, and deep furrows etched across her forehead and around the corners of her mouth.

"Girl," she sighed, "you're a wreck!"

She turned from the disturbing reflection and fumbled with the shower control. It had been like this three nights in a row. Each night the nightmare had been worse – more real, more deeply disturbing.

Diana stood in the stream of hot water staring vacantly at the rose-colored tile of her shower. She was tired – no, deeply exhausted – from lack of sleep. It seemed obvious that the dream had some deeper meaning, but her mind was too clouded with exhaustion to make sense of it. *In fact*, she thought, *nothing makes any sense lately. Not my job, my relationship…nothing. Feels like I'm just treading water – going exactly nowhere in my life.*

* * * * *

"Got to get it together," Diana sighed. She loosened the bottom of her blouse to camouflage the roll of flesh that pooched out above the waistband of her Gucci faded jeans, then wrestled into a too-tight matching jean jacket.

She glanced down at her bleached white sneakers and sighed at her choice of outfits. Still sighing, she selected a turquoise-studded silver watch and slid it onto her wrist. She contemplated her reflection in the full-length mirror, shook her head. "Gotta dress for the client, girl. You gotta…"

She folded her blue dressing gown and draped it over a chair, lifted a worn copy of *Path of Least Resistance* from the floor and placed it with the collection of books inside her prized, hand-rubbed white oak night stand, then made her bed with a practiced precision.

* * * * *

Diana slumped at the kitchen table – a half-eaten piece of dry toast, a cup of lukewarm English Breakfast tea, and a presentation folder in front of her. She stared vacantly at the toast, one finger absently tracing the embossed imprint on the crisp white linen folder: "Brody & Brody Advertising."

Three hours ten minutes to doomsday, she thought. She stared blankly at the folder – her sketches and design concepts for the GreenWatch "Plant A Tree" campaign.

Why am I so certain GreenWatch won't like my work? Why am I? Her job at Brody & Brody had somehow lost the excitement she had once felt at being a "real" graphic artist. *In fact,* she thought, *it's all starting to feel as shallow as my relationship with Jeff Brody. Doesn't anything have any meaning anymore? I feel like I'm just going through the motions.*

What's happened to me, she asked herself. Her logical mind insisted that she should be grateful to have a good job, a fairly decent post-divorce relationship, and...

She took a sip oft the lukewarm tea, winced at the tepid bitterness. "It's really true. Seems as though nothing has any meaning anymore," she sighed. "Like everything is just one big blah. I just haven't felt right ever since Jeff and I went to..."

The ecological catastrophe she'd discovered on her recent weekend trip to the Grand Canyon rushed into her memory. The smog was so thick they couldn't see to the other side of the canyon. Ever since, GreenWatch's predictions of an impending global environmental collapse had lurked like a hungry jackal around the edges of her mind.

Suddenly she realized – the sinister nightmare that had tortured her the past three nights, the terrifying dragon threatening to torch her to death, had first started that night in the campground by the canyon. *That's it.*

"That crazed nightmare has really scrambled my brains,"

she mumbled. She pushed her chair back and picked up the plate and cup, then grabbed the edge of the table as she tilted dangerously out of balance.

"Whoa. I've really got to get it together." Diana walked with forced steadiness to the sink, poured out the remaining cold tea, and washed the cup and toast plate.

The rest of the morning passed in a blur of intense mental exhaustion.

* * * * *

Diana rattled the doorknob of the back door of her Southern California Spanish-inspired house, its white stucco yellowed by too many years of the harsh LA sun and smog. "Gotta get this lock replaced, soon. Why is it that no matter what there's never enough money, or enough time?"

She kicked at a dead geranium that had collapsed onto the gravel walkway, its leaves thick with black smog soot. *And I need to get someone to clean up these weeds*, she thought. She glanced at her water-starved backyard, shook her head, and strode for the silver Tercel parked next to the house.

"Good morning," called an old woman from the porch of her cabin behind the next door house.

Diana looked over the fence, lifted her chin and forced a weak smile, then threw her briefcase on the passenger seat and climbed into the car.

Brother, she railed herself as she pulled the Tercel out onto the street. *That was just too rude of me. I really should be more neighborly. What's wrong with me lately?*

She stopped the car and backed up the driveway to apologize to her neighbor, then felt genuine disappointment to find that the old woman had gone back into her cabin. *I'll get her some flowers*, she promised.

* * * * *

Peter Tompson, founder of GreenWatch, dropped Diana's presentation folder on the conference table and pushed his chair back. He rose to his feet, hesitated, then blew out his breath explosively. "This just doesn't get me here," he said, poking his right index finger into his chest.

Diana blinked at the intense passion exploding from his hazel eyes. In a daze she followed his finger to the forest green T-shirt and the sunburst GreenWatch logo positioned on the right pocket – directly over his heart.

Tompson turned to Jeff Brody, senior partner of Brody & Brody. "This just isn't it, Jeff. Not even close."

I knew it, Diana thought. *I just knew it.* "Where did I fall short, Peter?" she asked softly.

"Cripes, Diana. Don't you see what's happening here? We really are just fiddling while Rome burns." He shook his head and paced to the window. "I don't know. Maybe you're typical of the very person we're trying to reach."

He strode back to the table, slapped his hand down on the presentation folder. "But one thing's for sure…this is definitely not what GreenWatch is after."

She blinked again at the fire radiating from his eyes.

"I can see you don't really believe in the importance of environmental activism do you, Diana?"

She leaned back in her chair to distance herself from him. "Well…yes. Yes I do, Peter."

He shook his head, blew out a puff of breath. "So, how are you involved?"

"Peter, not everyone can work as an activist." She forced a tight smile. "I mean–"

He impatiently cut her off. "So you don't feel the threat to our global environment is important?"

"Of course I do," she shrugged, "but what can I do?" "What can anyone do, really? The scientists are all telling us there's no hope and…" *Be cool girl,* she chided herself. *Just shut up. This is a major B&B client.*

An uneasy silence filled the room.

He looked at her silently, then shook his head. "My dear artist, if everyone had such an attitude of total helplessness there'd be no GreenWatch. And for sure, there'd be no hope!"

* * * * *

Diana tossed her briefcase into the back seat and leaned against the car. *Maybe he's right. Maybe I am totally out of touch,* she thought. She shook her head, checked the car door, then headed out along the arrows leading to the elevator.

She began the two block walk to Ming's where she and Jeff Brody had planned to share a victory dinner – her eyes smarting from the biting cocktail of smog and fresh exhaust rolling off the street.

Maybe I should move out of here, she thought. *This smog is getting to me. And all that violence last week in South Central and Hollywood...it's getting way too close.*

Diana leaned against the bamboo-papered wall in Ming's front entrance and waited for the hostess to seat her. *Gonna be some victory dinner,* she thought. *Jeff is going to be royally corked. And...I just trashed a good thirty hours designing a big time loser. Not good.*

* * * * *

The traffic had slogged into deadlock by the time Jeff Brody slid into the black lacquered Ming dynasty-inspired chair across from her.

"Sorry I'm late, honey." He exhaled roughly. "It took us a while to wrap up."

"It's OK, Jeff. So, does he want to see another approach?"

"Nope. Afraid not. Wants me to put another designer on the job."

"But Jeff," she protested, "I can–"

He shook his head to silence her. "Sorry Diana. It's just no go. He wants someone that's more actively involved."

Diana tightened her jaw, dropped her eyes, and let her breath out in a tightly controlled stream.

"Actively involved?" She shook her head. "Jeff, I'm a designer, not an enviro activist. What in blazes does he expect?"

"He's the client, Diana. And he feels your heart isn't into

9

the project." Brody looked down at the menu to signal that the discussion was closed.

Diana struggled to keep her face expressionless, fought the heaviness gathering in her chest "Look Jeff," she said softly. "I can't spend my time running around planting trees. I've got to make a living. But that doesn't mean I don't care about the environment. I really do, but–"

Brody looked up from the menu. "Let it go, Diana. He just doesn't feel you're in touch with GreenWatch's message. That's it. Period." He rested his forehead on his hand and focused on the menu.

"That's just not fair, Jeff." She choked back the lump in her throat.

He closed the menu and raised his eyebrows in obvious frustration. "Look, Diana. I'm really sorry but–"

"Jeff, please listen! Ever since we got back from the Grand Canyon I've…I've had this awful tightness around my heart. I know the rain forests are being wiped out. I know our water and food are poisoned…and downtown LA has turned into a war zone. Do you think I'm blind? Does he?"

"That's not the issue, Diana. You've got to see this as a professional and–"

"A professional? Look Jeff, I can see that the environment is collapsing around us. But what can I do? What can anyone do? Nothing makes any sense anymore."

She tightened her throat to choke back the threatening flood of tears.

Brody leaned forward and touched her forearm. "Hey, honey. You're really upset."

"Upset?" she choked. "I can't even sleep anymore Jeff. I keep having this horrible dream about a fire-breathing monster – a dragon – coming after me. Last night it woke me up three times. I think my whole life is spinning out of control. I really just don't know what to do." She buried her face in her hands.

Brody stared at her in obvious shock and dropped the menu onto his plate. "Forget dinner, Diana. Let's get out of here." He slid a five dollar bill under the edge of his plate, shoved back his chair and held his hand out to her.

They pushed out through the heavy carved wooden doors onto a sidewalk crammed with people, all surging in the same direction.

"Oh no," Diana moaned, "I forgot. The Chinese New Year's parade is tonight."

"Look, honey," he took her arm. "I've got to hit it before this crowd locks me in. Want me to walk you to your car?"

"No...just go for it," she sighed.

"Come on, I'll see you in two weeks when I get back from San Francisco. Why don't you take a week off, Diana. Don't worry. You'll do better on your next project."

"Sure," she shrugged. She braced her back against the front window of the restaurant and watched him struggle against the excited wave of parade goers.

The nervous tic that had tormented her right eyelid for two weeks returned. She pressed her palm against her eye to try to stop the irritating spasm.

"I'm really getting worn down," she muttered. "I just haven't had enough sleep." *I don't have the energy to fight this mob,* she admitted to herself. *Might as well just go see the stupid parade.*

She melted into the ocean of people pressing toward the parade route, hoping she could keep herself together.

* * * * *

Diana elbowed her way into the noisy, restless throng packed along the street. *This is probably a mistake*, she thought. *But here I am.*

"Hey," Diana gasped as a teenager roughly shoved her purple-haired companion against her. She watched in a daze as the top scoop of the girl's chocolate ice cream cone toppled off in her direction, splattered against the front of her white blouse, then slid down the leg of her Gucci jeans and landed on her left shoe.

The girl returned Diana's shocked look with a deadly, don't-mess-with-me, glare.

Suddenly a string of Chinese firecrackers exploded in the street. The sound snaked up Diana's spine and ended with a blinding red-orange flash in the very center of her brain. She staggered and lurched into the woman standing directly in front of her.

The woman spun around. "What," she snarled. She looked at the ice cream smeared on Diana's blouse and curled her upper lip in disgust. "Watch your step, street creep."

In the next instant a young boy in the front of the crowd twisted free from his mother's grip and bounded into the street. "Mommy," he shrieked, leaping up and down. "Here it comes.

The dragon…the dragon."

Diana felt a cold finger of anxiety slice through her at his words. She took a deep breath and rolled her shoulders to shake off the chilling sensation, then jostled for a better position to see over the heads of the boisterous crowd.

Five men dressed all in black led the parade – a tall firecracker pinwheel suspended high above their heads from bamboo poles. The poles were wrapped with strands of black crepe paper. The many-legged ceremonial dragon followed.

Diana tried to ignore a disturbing *deja vu* and focused on the dancers spinning around the dragon in wild abandon – their faces concealed by fearsome ceremonial masks. But the sensation of having already somehow experienced that very same moment persisted. *What does this remind me of?* She finally asked herself. *Everything seems to be moving so slow… almost too slow.*

The crowd pressed forward hoping to touch the dragon to ensure good luck for the coming year. Diana staggered and resisted, but was involuntarily carried along.

Suddenly the crowd separated, and she found herself trapped directly in the path of the dragon.

The exploding firecrackers, the amplified roar of the dragon, the lusty shouts of the crowd grew louder, then louder yet.

A bead of sweat formed on her upper lip and her ears began to ring. Diana looked around wild-eyed. There was no way to break free from the crowd.

She braced herself as the dragon danced closer, its long forked tongue reaching out to touch the bystanders.

In the instant the paper and wire tongue brushed against her arm Diana felt herself, almost dreamlike, begin to fall backward.

The exuberant shouts of the crowd, the unrestrained fervor of the dancers, echoed through a thick fog as though coming from miles away.

Then she heard a sickening, hollow thud as the back of her head slammed against the pavement like an overripe watermelon. She was vaguely aware of being enveloped in darkness, bathed in a strangely pulsating silence. Then nothing…

One foot after another stumbled over her as the many-legged dragon continued its twisting, snake-like dance down the street.

The instant the dragon passed three boys burst from the crowd and raced to claim her purse, now lying open in the street totally unprotected. The successful boy strutted proudly through the parade-goers displaying the purse above his head like a trophy. Another boy ripped the silver and turquoise watch from her wrist, then smashed it to the street when a larger boy with an orange-red mohawk challenged his rights of ownership.

A small crowd gathered around Diana's still body. A ragged pool of thick blood had formed around the back of her head in the form of a rough halo. Her clothes were filthy and

14

torn. One of her shoes had disappeared.

The crowd disbursed without comment or further interest when a tall cop brusquely elbowed his way into the crowd, lifted her off the street by her armpits, dragged her to the sidewalk, then punched a button on his cell phone to call for an ambulance.

* * * * *

The metallic taste of fresh blood.

A roaring fire-pain in the back of her head.

Blinding lights that passed right through her closed eyelids.

Diana struggled to clear her mind – to understand the voices around her. She finally gave up and focused mindlessly on the mushrooming patterns of light floating across the inside of her eyelids.

* * * * *

A dark-haired ER intern grabbed a hypodermic from a nurse's outstretched hand, then roughly jammed it into Diana's left arm.

"ID? Family?" A green-clad nurse asked the cop.

"Nope. No ID on her."

"Another Jane Doe," the nurse announced briskly to no one in particular. She scribbled a note on a form, then deftly slid the metal clipboard under Diana's shoeless foot.

* * * * *

The frenzied sounds and brilliant lights of the emergency room drifted farther and farther away as the injection took hold. Diana felt herself grow heavier – begin sink deeper down into the gurney.

Then a sudden sharp pop shattered her drugged calmness.

She struggled to focus her vision – discovered she was floating just beneath the ceiling in the far corner of the emergency room. *Everything seems so clear and bright*, she noted with unusual clarity. She focused on the body lying very still on the gurney below her, and calmly recognized it as herself.

Diana watched dreamlike from the ceiling as a nurse cut hair away from the deep gash in the back of her head. Another nurse stood next to her, catching the blood soaked auburn hair in a plastic wastebasket.

She saw the dark-haired intern bend over and peel back her right eyelid, and watched her own hand fly involuntarily at his face.

The intern grabbed her forearm roughly. "Phew. Get some restraints on this nut case," he growled. "Run skull pictures – back and temporal. Cervical spine too…and get a baseline EEG. Clean her up and get her out of here," he barked at the older nurse.

The nurse grabbed the clipboard. "Diagnosis?" she asked.

"Probable brain trauma. Needs observation."

Suddenly the sounds of the emergency room were replaced by a loud hissing sound in her forehead

Diana thought she saw a small rectangular door swing open somewhere above her. Then an uncomfortably familiar green light burst from the door-like opening, tore directly at her, and splattered against the crown of her head.

The emergency room immediately disappeared.

Diana found herself catapulting head first into a tunnel darker than the darkest night.

For a moment she thought she heard birds singing…then her sense of consciousness dissolved into the darkness.

CR80

CHAPTER TWO

Every myth is somehow based on fact.

—Joseph Campbell

DIANA'S EYELIDS FLUTTERED, then opened briefly to a soothing light and the sound of birdsong. A warm, moisture rich breeze played across her naked body. The pungent odor of aged humus filled her nostrils.

She pulled in a deep breath. The scent reminded her of the soil and bark mixture her uncle had used to pot his prize orchids. As a child she had mixed the bark and humus for him in a heavy glass cup marked with fine red lines and numbers – the musty aromatic soil to the third line, then the reddish bark to the top of the cup. She could hear his voice. "*All the way to the top now…to the top.*"

She sighed deeply and curled her fingertips into the lush richness beneath her; but her reverie was suddenly interrupted by a nagging voice in the back of her head. *Something's not right*, it insisted. *Not right, not right…*

A sense of sick dizziness overtook her. She shuddered as an uninvited vision of herself in a stark white room slammed into her consciousness.

She became aware of herself lying motionless on a hard bed. A tall woman dressed in white was securing tight restraints over her wrists. A second woman, also dressed in white, was attaching electronic sensors to her forehead.

In her vision Diana saw the tall woman – a nurse? – swab the inside of her right forearm with an alcohol-soaked wad of cotton. She saw her own fingers twitch as the woman expertly inserted a long needle into her arm. Diana ran her eyes along the length of the plastic tube attached to the end of the needle. It was connected to a bottle of clear fluid hanging from a polished chrome stand.

The instant the first drop of the cold fluid entered her vein, a deep muscular spasm erupted from her sacrum and blasted its way up the full length of her spine.

The unwelcome vision was replaced by deeply soothing sounds of birdsong and gently moving water.

* * * * *

The young woman parted the Tua vines to explore the odd white spot that had caught her eye through the dense jungle foliage.

Her jaw dropped.

Lying in a small sunlit clearing was a totally naked

unconscious woman. "Marieji," she shouted. "Marieji, come here. Quick."

Her companion, a lithe, deeply tanned silver-haired woman, knelt and lightly touched the naked woman's wrist to check for a pulse.

"Go. Bring help," she commanded.

The younger woman threw down her gathering bag and bounded toward a well-worn path.

"Sola," the silver-haired woman called out after her younger companion. "Bring a stretcher."

The woman unwrapped the earth-colored cloth tied loosely around her shoulder and waist and draped it over the naked woman's body. She then picked a large leaf from a flowering tree, rolled the leaf into a funnel, and slipped through some overhanging vines to a small pool of water.

The silver-haired woman returned and squatted down next to the motionless body. Shaking her head, she gently directed a tiny rivulet of cool water onto the stranger's lips and cheeks, then across her forehead.

"Marieji? Where are you?" a male voice called out.

"Here." The silver-haired woman stood up to guide the caller to her. "Over here"

Two men wearing only tan shorts crashed through the thick foliage – one carrying two long poles, the other a blanket. The shorter of the two men quickly rolled the long edge of the blanket around one pole, then looped the rest of the blanket around the other pole to form a simple stretcher.

"Go find Olji," the silver-haired woman ordered the

younger woman as she joined them. "Have her meet us at the visitors' huts. And have her bring her medicine bag, Sola."

The men carried Diana into the largest of a cluster of three grass huts in a small clearing. Following the older woman's directions, they deposited her limp body onto a small bed fashioned of bamboo and tightly woven vines.

* * * * *

The silver-haired woman and her companion silently watched Olji, the village's slender, ebony-skinned master healer, at work.

The healer put an ear to Diana's chest, then placed two long, finely tapered fingers onto the side of her neck. Satisfied with the pulse, she expertly slipped her hands beneath the lower part of Diana's back and slowly slid them up her spine to investigate each vertebrae. She nodded her head, then gently pressed her fingertips into the muscles of Diana's neck and shoulders.

"Deep neck sprain, Marieji," Olji commented. "But no broken or fractured bones. Except for the skull, that is."

The healer moved to the head of the bed and glanced over at the younger woman. "Sola, could you please hand me that basin and water?"

They watched Olji deftly crop the hair around the stranger's head wound with a razor-sharp knife, then flood it with rivulets of warm water squeezed from a white cloth.

The younger woman nervously ran her fingers through her

own hair as she watched the water in the basin turn red with blood. She turned to her older companion.

"Do you think she fell through the gate, Marieji?"

"Without a doubt," the silver-haired woman nodded. "How else could she get here, Sola?"

"Do you think she stands a chance? Of returning, I mean."

"You remember what happened to the last three who fell through the dragon's gate, don't you?"

The young woman set her jaw.

"Then you realize what an overwhelming challenge this woman faces. Does she look like a warrior to you?"

"Not at all, Marieji. What will you do with her?"

"The only thing I can do. Encourage her to step onto the warrior's path. Then hope she has the courage to claim her own power."

"I can't imagine how it must feel to someone like her… to have to change so rapidly. How do you ever make warriors of them, Marieji?"

"I don't. They must make warriors of themselves, Sola. And as you know, it takes great passion and courage. And then, to face that final moment of truth–"

"The wound will heal in a couple of weeks with this," the healer interrupted. She held up a flattened stick covered with bright yellow salve, then smeared the salve onto a neatly folded white cloth dressing. "Except for a headache from the head blow, that is. But she has suffered a deep mental shock," she continued. "More than what shows on the surface."

The healer positioned the dressing and wrapped a soft cloth bandage around Diana's head. "She may not focus well enough to survive, Marieji. I suggest someone stay the night with her."

Marieji glanced at Sola, who nodded her head in silent understanding.

Sola stood watch throughout the night while Diana slept an alternately too restless, and too quiet, sleep.

* * * * *

The morning dawned as each new day begins in the dense jungle at the Western Gate of Gaia. First there was a pause – a stillness as the night birds fell silent just before the sky began to lighten.

Then, in the very instant the first shaft of sunlight streaked across the eastern sky, the Morning Parrot threw open its huge tangerine beak and shrieked an unmistakable wake-up command.

The entire jungle exploded into a boisterous tango. Monkeys threw themselves from the trees and bounded into the village to beg for breakfast scraps; birds scattered to their favorite hunting grounds; insects crawled from their hiding places to resume their endless search for food.

* * * * *

Marieji pulled aside the door net and entered the hut soundlessly. She lifted her chin to dismiss Sola, then went to the bed and placed her fingers lightly on Diana's wrist.

Satisfied, she glided to the low stool next to the door and settled in to watch the morning unfold.

* * * * *

Diana was aware of the riotous awakening of the jungle as though from a long way off. A deafening headache pounded at the inside of her skull, and a survival-level demand for immediate, full awareness scratched insistently at the back of her mind. *Wake up*, it demanded.

She forced her eyes open, then gasped as the unexpected sight of the domed ceiling of the grass hut ripped the remaining sleep from her.

She jerked upright, then collapsed over herself in pain, her hands holding her bandage-wrapped head. *This is not right.* The words echoed through her mind. *Not right, not right, not right…*

Like a wild animal, Diana suddenly became aware of the presence of another person in the room. Her eyes raced around the hut, landing on the silver-haired woman who sat silently on the low stool watching her.

"What?" She rubbed her eyes, then felt dizzy as her mind raced from confusion, to madness, to denial, and finally settled into deep shock.

The silver-haired woman continued to stare at her, unblinking.

"Who," Diana stammered. "Who are you?" She felt her eyes bulge with a sudden memory. "Wait. I remember a… a hospital?" She shuddered as the other woman rose silently, walked over to her, then bent over and gently pushed her back down onto the bed.

"My head," Diana moaned. "What happened to me? Where am I?"

"You're safe. You've just lost your way and–"

"Lost my way? What? What do you mean?"

"You'll be OK. Just relax. Part of you is lost…in what could be a deep coma. But we can help you deal with–"

"Coma?" Diana pushed the woman's hand off her shoulder. "What? What have you done to me?"

"Nothing has been done to you," Marieji said softly. She placed a finger lightly on her own forehead. "It all starts here."

"Oh sure," Diana snorted through her pain. "This is all in my mind."

"That's a good start," Marieji replied. "But rest for now. I'll bring food."

Now totally unsettled, Diana sought desperate refuge behind closed eyes and forced sleep.

* * * * *

Her attempt at sleep was interrupted by a vaguely familiar voice asking her name. She felt part of herself rise upward as though from the bottom of some murky, featureless sea.

"Diana," she heard herself say thickly. "My name is… Diana."

Her focus improved. Diana found the same silver-haired woman standing before her – a tray of food balanced easily in one hand, and a yellow fiber canteen in the other.

"You," Diana stammered. Her hand went involuntarily to the bandage wrapped around her head. "Where am I?"

"Eat. Then we'll talk."

The aroma of the fresh bread and hot soup overrode her anxiety. Diana watched the other woman out of the corner of her eye during her first few bites, then lost herself in the food. She drank the last of the hot broth, then looked at the delicate yellow and white fleshed fruit she had just bitten into. "What fruit is this?"

"It's from the Sayto tree. Do you like it?"

Diana nodded appreciation, took another bite, then suddenly dropped the remainder of the fruit onto the tray and looked up.

Am I still asleep? she asked herself. She looked down at the back of her hand to check her reality and saw the familiar white scar from a childhood playground accident. *I'm not asleep. So I must be awake.*

The older woman cleared her throat and waited.

"Say...to tree?" Diana looked around the hut, then stared intensely at the silver-haired woman. "You look real enough," she said slowly. "But this...this has to be some kind of drug-caused hallucination. I remember a hospital bed, and–"

"You're not hallucinating."

Diana felt the muscles in her face, neck and stomach convulse. A deep uneasiness settled over her. She stared at the silver-haired woman. *Psychiatrist,* she thought. *She must be a shrink.* Her eyes scanned the hut, suddenly locked on the dragon's head medallion hanging around the woman's neck. She felt the hair on her neck stand up. *A dragon's head?*

"This is no hospital," she gasped. "Where am I?"

"Hospital? No," the silver-haired woman replied. "But most certainly a place of healing."

"So," Diana winced. "I've totally lost it and...and I'm in the nut house. Right?" Diana glanced at the door. *A clear path of escape?*

In one desperate thrust she bolted off the bed and lunged toward the door of the hut, then dropped onto the low stool as her knees buckled. She stared in disbelief out the door.

"Oh no," she stammered. "There's a jungle out there." Diana spun to face the other woman, who stood looking at her with an irritating calmness. "Who are you?"

"Don't be afraid. My name is Marieji. Get some clothes on." She pointed to a neat pile of clothing on a small table against the wall of the hut. "Then we'll go down to the river. The fresh air will help clear your mind."

ଓଃୠ

CHAPTER THREE

Am I a man dreaming I'm a butterfly?
Or a butterfly dreaming I'm a man?

—Gautama Buddha

DIANA FOLLOWED THE silver-haired woman out onto the
sun-flooded beach, eyes smarting from the intense light that
ricocheted off the water and white sand. She shaded her eyes
and scanned the dark jungle on the other side of the river. She
could count her heartbeats by the painful throb in the back of
her head.

Marieji settled lightly onto the sand in the full sun.
"Beautiful, isn't it? Sit." She pointed a deeply tanned finger
to a spot on the sand just in front of her.

"Do I have a choice?" Diana muttered. She cautiously
eased herself down onto the warm sand, then turned her
attention inward. Her mind was being tormented by a

disturbing sensation of being pulled in two totally opposite directions at the same time.

Marieji stretched her arms above her head and rolled her shoulders, then looked curiously at Diana. "Does your head hurt? Take a deep breath," she smiled. "Just try to let your neck and shoulders relax."

Diana looked up at the woman she now knew as Marieji. *Funny name,* she thought. *Something really odd about her. About this whole place. They must have drugged me. How else could they bring me to this jungle?* "What country is this?" Diana rasped. "Why did you bring me here? And–"

"You're in the jungle at the Western Gate of Gaia. The river you see before you is called the Western River."

Diana considered the older woman's words, then frowned and shook her head. *If I can get a straight answer, maybe I can figure out how to get out of here* "Gaia. Is that African? Or is this South America? Since this obviously isn't a hospital, I guess I've been kidnapped, right? Look, if it's money you're after..."

Marieji laughed down deep in her throat. "Please...please just allow me to explain."

Diana sighed. She was getting nowhere with this old woman. It was probably a strategy to totally confuse her. "Do I have a choice?" she snapped.

"We always have choices. That's up to you. Just let me explain. First, you need to know you won't find this jungle on any map of Earth."

Right. Next she'll insist that the world is really flat. "Fat chance," Diana snarled. "I'm on the moon, right? Can't we just get to the point of this cute little kidnapping game."

"This isn't a game Diana, and no one brought you here against your will. You came here on your own."

"Oh brother," Diana spat. "And I suppose I also broke my own skull open."

"We don't know how you were injured, but I can–"

"Look Marie...What's your name again?"

"Marieji."

"Look, Marieji. Just tell me what you people want."

A long silence.

Time seemed to stretch out oddly. Diana watched the other woman look back at her with troubled eyes.

Marieji finally shook her head slowly. "Are you ready to listen?"

Diana looked at her without speaking. She swallowed hard. Her throat was tight and raw. Everything felt extremely strange and somehow out of sync. "OK," she finally shrugged. "So just tell me, where am I...really?"

"You are not on what you understand to be Earth, although we know it to be the same planet. You have brought yourself to Gaia."

Diana felt her jaw go slack. Her head hurt even more. *Oh boy. Is this Marieji totally loony, or what? This can't be happening,* her inner self protested. "Not real, not real, not..." she mumbled softly.

The older woman sat for a moment without speaking. "Do you understand what I'm saying, Diana?" she finally said.

"Oh sure," Diana laughed nervously. *This isn't really happening*, she reassured herself. *Can't be.* A burning sensation spread from her neck up onto her face. An irritating buzz filled her head – like a hive of bees in a tree trunk.

"Are you certain you understand?"

Diana stared into the bright shards of light dancing off the surface of the river. She struggled with how she had ended up in the jungle. *Is this really a jungle?* she pondered. *Maybe I've been drugged. This whole thing could very well just be a nasty hallucination. Or am I being held hostage?*

She suddenly realized that the older woman had used the term "Gaia" – the same term GreenWatch used to refer to the Earth as a living, conscious being. *That's it,* she decided. *This Marieji is obviously playing with my mind.*

Marieji reached out and touched Diana's foot. "Do you understand what I'm saying?"

"You bet I understand. You're testing me to see if I'm nuts enough to take what you're saying at face value. But why are you…"

"No, Diana. This isn't a test, as you put it. I'm speaking the simple truth."

Diana stared into the woman's crisp blue eyes. She didn't seem to be lying. A rush of fear twisted her stomach and pushed a vile taste up into her mouth. It seemed as though the sky was falling and the ground coming up to meet her at the same time. She wrapped her arms around her knees and started to rock.

"Diana?"

She focused on the slap of the river water against the beach, matching the rhythmic sound with her rocking motion. "Not true, not true, not true…" she reassured herself.

31

"Diana, I realize this is a deep shock. But what I've told you is in fact the truth."

Diana blankly watched her own emotions splatter against some imaginary wall, then explode out of control. Fear, confusion, madness, and finally denial swept through her. *Wake up*, a voice inside her mind screamed. *Got to wake up.*

She shook her head and was immediately sorry. Intense pain jammed through her head, her neck, and down into her shoulders. *Not a dream. Too real.*

She turned her attention to the silver-haired woman she now knew as Marieji. "Why did you say that this…this place is not on Earth?"

"Diana, both places are tied to what you call Earth. But Earth and Gaia each exist in a different vibratory frequency – something like two different notes on the same musical scale."

Diana resumed her rocking with even greater intensity. *I've got to wake up. I'm in no condition to handle this.* She jammed down on the muscles in her jaw and throat to choke back the intense emotions flooding her mind.

Marieji stood up and walked to the river, filled a leaf with water, brought it back and silently offered it to Diana.

Diana took the water-filled leaf in both hands, studied it blankly, then poured the water out on the sand.

"Look," she protested. "I know you've drugged me. I remember a hospital. Somebody stuck a needle in my arm, and…I'm betting this jungle isn't even real."

Marieji sighed and slowly shook her head. "No one has drugged you, Diana. And I can reassure you, both this jungle and Gaia are just as real as Earth."

"I really doubt it. And just who are you anyway? And what do you want from me?"

"You'll come to understand who I am. And I don't want anything from you," Marieji replied. "Let me explain how you probably found your way here to Gaia."

Diana hesitated and looked deeply into the woman's eyes again. The warmth of the sun on her body was definitely real. She fingered the bandage wrapped around her head. *Not a dream. Too real.* She shrugged her shoulders. "OK. So let's have it."

Marieji returned her gaze silently and steadily. "Good. We'll start with the relationship of Gaia to Earth. This will help you."

The sensation of being simultaneously pulled in two different directions sliced through the back of her mind again. *Yes…help*, Diana cried out silently. *Please, help.*

Marieji smoothed the sand with her hand, then picked up a small stick and drew a circle. "This is the core – the heart – of Earth." She hesitated and looked up to confirm Diana's attention.

Diana involuntarily choked back an odd sound that sounded to her like an animal in pain.

"And these are the energy bands surrounding that core." Marieji drew several increasingly larger circles around the first circle. "Each circle is like an adjacent layer of skin, just like the layered skins of an onion."

Diana bent forward and looked back and forth from the drawing to Marieji. The light had suddenly shifted. Everything seemed oddly magnified, almost like the time she had taken

LSD as a college sophomore. *This all feels sort of ultra real,* she thought.

"Now suppose each of these circles is a skin of the same onion," Marieji continued. "But if you were a little bug sitting on this skin," she poked the end of the stick into the inner circle representing Earth, "you might not realize the other skins were out there." She looked at Diana intently. "Do you follow me?"

"Yeah. I think so, but…" *Wonder who she really is? Onion skins?*

"Suppose one day that bug found a hole leading to the next skin out and crawled up through it. What would he find?"

As Marieji drew a line connecting the center circle with the next circle out, a barely conscious sensation of familiarity flowed through the back of Diana's mind.

"That little bug might think it was on an entirely different world – although in truth, it was just standing on another skin of the very same onion," Marieji said.

"Huh," Diana exclaimed.

Marieji looked at Diana thoughtfully for a moment. "But if the bug remembered how he got there, of course, he could just crawl back through the hole and be home again."

Diana choked on a nervous laugh.

"In fact Earth and Gaia are like different layers of the same onion," Marieji continued. "You might say we are different dimensions of the same living planet. Our realities are certainly molded by the same forces."

An interesting theory, Diana thought. "But what do you mean, molded by the same forces?" she asked.

Marieji shifted her weight and looked straight into Diana's eyes. "Diana. this jungle had its beginning in your very layer of the onion. It was a small part of a great continent covered by large bodies of water, a rich savanna, and a great rain forest. My ancestors were among the survivors of the ecological catastrophes that began during what your people will soon refer to as Earth's Great Change."

"Ecological catastrophes? Uhh." Diana set her teeth. "That sounds too familiar for comfort. But if I'm on another skin of the onion, what are you trying to tell me – that I'm really dead?"

"No, you are definitely alive. You've done what that little bug did, except that you left your physical body back on Earth. The focal point of your consciousness somehow slipped through what we call the dragon's gate – a vortex of energy connecting our two worlds. Diana, you are in a different vibratory frequency that may seem like another world to you, or even the future."

"The future?"

"Yes. But actually, your Earth and my Gaia are basically simultaneous. We are often visited by fleeting images of people from your Earth in their dream state – our vibratory levels are very, very close. But in your case, it's as though you have truly become your dream."

Diana bent over the drawing, then looked up at Marieji. It seemed clear that the woman thought she was speaking the truth. She struggled to get a grip on something she could solidly identify as reality. *From one layer of an onion to another? Could such a thing be possible? Could she be speaking the truth? And the dream – could the dragon be…*

"But what do you mean," Diana stammered, "left my body?"

"You are only weakly anchored here on Gaia, Diana. Some intense trauma must have broken your connection with Earth's vibratory frequency. I can't say why this happens. Many shamans and master teachers and mystics visit us on purpose. The ancient Earth brother Babaji comes often; but you didn't leave your physical body on purpose. In fact, it's very likely in grave danger."

Diana looked down at her right hand. "Can't be true." She pinched a fold of skin on the back of her hand. "My body is right here."

"A Gaia body."

"Hey. This looks like the same body to me," Diana protested.

"It looks like the same body because that's what you expect to see, and therefore what your mind creates. Once you learn to look with a deeper vision, you'll realize that you really have many, many overlapping bodies. But for now we need to concentrate on the challenge you face. For the core of your being is still tied to your Earth body, and is very likely withering in a coma."

"Withering? In a coma?" The skin of Diana's face stretched tight. *This isn't entertaining, not even a little bit.*

Marieji hesitated, shifted her weight, then looked Diana full in the eyes. "Please listen to me. I have no reason to lie to you. You have a limited time. Your life as the person you call Diana depends on the survival of the body you obviously left behind untended."

"That's just great. So how do I get back?"

"You must return home the same way you came – through the dragon's gate connecting your dimension and Gaia."

"Dragon's gate?" *Here we go again. This woman has to be a nut case.* Diana choked back a river of bile threatening to explode up into her throat. "Look," she spat. "I don't know who you are, but I'm not into playing your fairy tale games."

Marieji studied her silently, then erased the sand drawing with her hand. "I've spoken the truth. To return you'll have to step onto the warrior's path – prepare yourself for a great moment of truth."

"Warrior's path?" Diana moaned. "Oh brother, have I managed to get myself into a–"

Marieji suddenly leapt to her feet, grabbed a huge stick, then forcefully smashed the stick to the ground right next to Diana's leg.

Diana jumped to her feet as the stick shattered into three pieces. "What in blazes was that for?" she bellowed. "You could have broken my leg."

Marieji squatted down and pointed to a faint trace in the sand leading toward where Diana had been sitting. "Do you see this trail? You were about to have an encounter with a very deadly snake."

She tossed aside the remaining piece of the broken stick, then calmly settled down onto the sand and pointed to a spot directly in front of her. "Sit."

"Deadly? You mean it could have killed me?" Diana circled like a cat before she finally sat back down onto the sand. "I hate snakes," she shuddered. "Creepy."

"Yet you chose to interpret my action as an attack against you. True?"

Diana nodded agreement. "Yeh, I guess I did."

"So the reality you created was that I was threatening your life, rather than trying to save it?"

Diana shrugged and looked fearfully at the thick jungle underbrush surrounding them. "Are there a lot of poisonous snakes around here?"

"Oh yes," Marieji nodded. "This is a place of many varied lifeforms. The viper you almost encountered is bright green – the color of the sun shining through the Ponga tree leaves. She has a brilliant red stripe around her neck. You'll likely see her again."

Diana sucked in a ragged breath and wrapped her arms tightly around her knees, pulling her feet up close.

Marieji put a finger to her mouth to signal for silence. "Here's a lesson for you. Watch." She cupped one hand and began to chant and drum rhythmically on the sand. Her body swayed slowly back and forth in a hypnotic motion.

Diana stared transfixed. The sun reflecting off Marieji's silver hair created the impression of a shimmering halo of energy around her head. Her entire body seemed to glow, and faintly colored overlapping rings of energy wrapped around the older woman.

She looked to Diana to be both ancient, and tremendously powerful.

Still swaying and drumming on the sand, Marieji suddenly opened her eyes and pointed to the underbrush a few feet from Diana.

Diana turned to look where she had pointed. A brilliant green snake emerged from the brush – its slender body the full length of her arm. A vivid red stripe circled its neck.

"Don't move," Marieji whispered.

The snake's head moved hypnotically to the rhythm Marieji still drummed on the sand – its tongue flicking in and out as it explored its environment.

"Beautiful." Marieji whispered. "Don't move, Diana. You're not in danger."

Diana held her breath as the snake slithered closer to Marieji.

"Now watch," Marieji said softly. She stopped drumming, gently placed the back of her hand on the sand directly in front of the snake, then slowly opened her fingers until they almost touched the viper's head.

Diana set her teeth as the snake stopped, reached out to explore Marieji's hand with its forked tongue, then crawled up onto her open palm and wrapped itself into a tight coil, resting its wedge-shaped head comfortably on Marieji's thumb.

"Twoo, twoo, twoo," Marieji crooned. She briefly stroked the viper's head with a single finger, then gently slid it back onto the warm sand.

The snake uncoiled and slithered off toward the river.

"I thought you said that snake was poisonous," Diana exploded.

Marieji laughed "Oh indeed it is. Its venom can easily kill a fully grown man."

"So why? How did you–"

"Diana, the viper is either harmless or deadly. It depends

on how you choose to respond to its presence. It's all up to you."

"But you said it was a killer."

"Only if you choose to be her prey. There's an important lesson here, Diana. We literally create our reality with our attitudes and expectations. It's not what happens to you that's important. It's how you choose to *respond* to what happens that creates what we call reality."

"*Creates* reality?"

"Diana. There are no accidents. We each create and attract virtually everything that happens to us. You must realize, for example, that somewhere within yourself you had a deep desire to stand in the face of the dragon...or you wouldn't even be here."

Dragon? Diana cringed as the terrible nightmare that had tortured her sleep flooded into her mind. *How could she know about the beast in my dream?*

Marieji stood and extended a hand to Diana. "You'll come to understand. But let's return to the hut. You need food, and a lot more rest."

Marieji laughed as she pulled aside the door net. "Ah, I see Olji has sent a friend to help you heal."

A Siamese cat lying on the bed pinned Diana with curious blue eyes.

"Hello Chat Chew," Marieji bowed her head to the cat.

"Me...ee...ow." The cat stood and arched its back as Marieji scratched behind its ears.

Marieji turned to Diana. "Olji will be here soon to change

your bandage. And food will follow."

Diana settled onto the bed next to the cat, who promptly pushed her head against Diana's hand in an unmistakable feline demand for attention.

"Rest well." Marieji pulled aside the door net to leave. "In the morning we'll speak of how to best use the time before your Earth body dies."

Before my body dies? Diana surged to her feet and ripped open the door net. But Marieji was gone, swallowed by the darkening jungle. That same sinister darkness had begun to creep across the clearing and gather around the hut itself.

Diana sucked in a deep breath and tried to focus beyond her fear. *There must be a way out of here. I can make a run for it.* She shook off the chill that crept into her mind and retreated back to the bed. *Run to where? Out into that creepy jungle?*

CHAPTER FOUR

*From the standpoint of immortality, we may have
a body within a body to infinity. When this physical body
is no longer a fit instrument through which to function,
another one may be already there.*

—*Ernest Holmes*

A GROUP OF residents stood around the bed, oblivious of the nurse who was busy checking the tangled assortment of electronic wires attached to Diana's skull.

The nurse painstakingly inspected the sensor pads one at a time, then traced each connector wire to its multi-channel EEG connector jack. She clicked her tongue, removed one sensor pad, then applied a dab of thick gel paste to Diana's shaved skull and applied a fresh pad.

"As you can see," explained first year medical resident Katie White, a youngish woman with cropped blond hair and intense blue eyes, "I'm running a 32-channel EEG. She's one of three comatose patients I'm currently studying." White hesitated to clear her throat. "The upper half of the screen displays her current readings, the lower half her average readings to date. Not currently displayed are the separate analyses of her beta, alpha, theta and delta range readings."

Another resident turned to the older doctor who stood slightly apart from the group. "What's the prognosis, Dr. Brennan?"

"Not sure yet," responded LA New Community Hospital's Chief of Surgery, Doctor Charles Brennan, in a flat matter-of-fact tone. "Obviously comatose. We'll give her another 72 hours. If there aren't any distinct improvements, we're putting her up for exploratory brain surgery."

"Family?" asked one of the other residents.

"No ID on her at admission," Brennan shrugged. "Street person. Good teaching case."

"Great," smiled a dark-haired resident standing at the foot of the bed.

Two of the other residents looked openly surprised at his obvious enthusiasm. Brennan crossed his arms and glared at them. "You two have some problem with this? It's a high risk procedure; but you doctors are here to practice, aren't you?"

"Dr. Brennan," resident White asked cautiously. "Her brainwaves are very unusual – not at all like the other two comatose patients. If I could just have a little more time to–"

"You've got the same 72 hours, White."

CHAPTER FIVE

Take time by the forelock…
find your eternity in each moment.

—*Henry David Thoreau*

THE SHRIEK OF the Morning Parrot shattered her sleep. Diana blinked away the fluorescent blue spots dancing in front of her eyes, then remembered–

The jungle. That strange woman – Marieji.

She rolled onto her side and looked out through the door net. *Jungle, still there.* She reached with one hand to explore her head. *Bandage still there too.*

The shrill cry of the parrot repeated and was answered by a rowdy mix of chatters and screeches. Diana slid her legs out from beneath the bed cover, then forced herself upright on the edge of the bed. She gasped as pain jammed hot and intense into her neck and right shoulder.

A bright patch of color on the table caught her attention. *A basket of fruit?* Bone level hunger pulled her off the bed and onto her feet. Diana sucked in a deep breath to steady herself and shuffled toward the table with uneven steps.

She selected a deep red soft-skinned fruit, bit into it, and was rewarded with an explosion of sweet nectar. She turned her attention to the neatly folded cocoa brown shorts and matching tunic next to the basket. A note was tucked into the pocket of the tunic. "Follow the path to the river and bathe," it read.

Diana finished the fruit and contemplated the other items on the table – a toothbrush made from the stem of a plant, one end split into brush-like fibers; a straw-colored woven towel; and a hand-shaped bar of peach-colored soap. Then with a designer's sensitivity to detail she inspected the soapmaker's imprint pressed into the center of the bar, also admiring the light floral scent.

She steadied herself on the table and pulled on the shorts and tunic, then slipped on the sturdy woven sandals Marieji had given her the day before. She pushed away from the table, but immediately grabbed the edge for support as a sudden wave of nausea rolled over her.

Just then the Siamese cat that had slept the night with her abruptly flew through the door net – a large scarlet-bellied lizard dangling from its mouth. The cat casually dropped the lizard at Diana's feet, sauntered across the hut, paused for a luxurious stretch, then jumped up onto the bed.

"Oh great," Diana gasped. "Just what I need. A dinosaur-sized lizard." *I've got to get out of this creepy jungle. Fast!*

There's got to be a way out of here, she reassured herself.

The cat rested its head comfortably on outstretched paws and watched through half-closed eyes as Diana grabbed the soap and towel and quickly slid toward the door, her back pressed solidly against the wall of the hut.

Diana stood on the porch and surveyed the dark jungle. What had Marieji said? *If that little bug just crawled back through the same hole…* "This is all too strange," she muttered. "But, if what she said is really true, I can just go back the way I came. I've got to figure out how, fast."

The sudden laughter of children, the cry of a baby, the sharp barking of a dog in the village proper, startled her out of her reverie. "OK self," she sighed. "Pay attention. I'll find the way out of here, and I'll do it today."

Diana pulled in a deep breath, exhaled slowly, then headed for the clearly marked trail she knew from yesterday led to the river. She moved cautiously onto the jungle path, lurching backward when a reddish brown blur catapulted from a tree and landed directly in front of her on the path.

"Just a monkey," she reassured herself. "Gotta get a grip on my nerves."

A parrot shrieked and sliced through the thick air just above her head. Diana shivered at the memory of the bright green viper that had crawled onto Marieji's hand. *Geez,* she thought. *This place really is just far too creepy.*

* * * * *

Diana heard voices and loud laughter even before she stepped from beneath the thick jungle canopy out onto the sunny beach.

A tall, brown-skinned man stood waist-deep in the river shaking water from his hair. Two young boys sat on the sand wrapped in towels.

She headed upstream toward what seemed to be the women's end of the beach. She forced herself knee-deep into the cool water just downstream from a small group of tanned women who laughed and splashed in the water as though it were bathtub temperature.

A fluorescent green beetle landed on her arm, then dove off into the water – reminding her again of Marieji's snake. She washed herself quickly, deeply relieved that none of the women seemed to notice her.

* * * * *

"Phoo," Diana spat as she stepped out of the jungle into the clearing in front of the visitors' huts. Seated on the porch in the sun, was Marieji – obviously waiting for her. "Oh well," she sighed. *Maybe I can pull some more information out of her. Figure out the best way to get the blazes out of this crazed place.*

"Feeling better today?" Marieji asked.

Diana shrugged her shoulders. Pain jabbed at the pit of her stomach. "OK. But I'm really hungry."

Marieji patted the wooden porch. "Sit. I brought you some hot food."

Diana settled onto the porch and accepted the cobalt blue glazed clay bowl. She lifted the wooden lid and discovered hot cereal, accepted the polished wooden spoon Marieji held out to her, and ate eagerly.

"How is your head, Diana?"

"OK, I guess."

When Diana placed the empty bowl down on the porch, Marieji immediately stood and held out a deeply tanned hand. "Come with me. I want to take you to a special place to explore the challenge you face."

* * * * *

Diana stumbled to a stop and peeled the sweat-soaked tunic away from her chest and back. She watched blankly as Marieji bowed to the tall waterfall she had led her to, then dropped to one knee and splashed water onto her face. Diana squatted and threw the cool water onto her own face and neck.

"Do you need to rest?" Marieji asked.

She scanned the older woman's face. The intense hike had left no signs of exertion – only a deep rosiness in the woman's cheeks. Hating to reveal her own exhaustion, she hesitated, then sat down on the sun-warmed sand.

Marieji settled onto the sand facing her and sat silently. "Diana," she finally said. "We need to capture the details of your passage through the gate while it's still clear in your mind."

Diana laid the palms of her hands down on the sand to absorb the warmth, then pressed them against the back of her neck. The deep throbbing in her head was relentless.

"Why don't you lie back on the sand," Marieji suggested. "Just listen to the sound of the river and relax."

She eased herself back onto the sand and felt her resistance dissolve into the comforting warmth. *So good just to lie in the sun,* she admitted. She released her breath gently in a long, deep sigh. She would worry about how to escape later. Later...

"Good, Diana. Now sleep...dream...and remember," Marieji intoned in a low voice.

For a moment Diana thought she saw a headband of brightly colored parrot feathers around the older woman's forehead. Then she closed her eyes, melted into the soothing comfort of the warm sand, and surrendered into a deep, trance-like sleep.

The dreams came instantly. Frame-by-frame in slow motion Diana saw, heard, and felt herself being pushed into the path of the ceremonial dragon. But then in the moment the paper and wire tongue brushed against her arm, her dream was shattered by a vision of a different dragon – this one spitting out very real fireballs that torched everything in its path.

The brief vision of the fire-breathing dragon was erased by the sick thud of her head as it slammed against the street. In her dream she wept to feel her blood flowing onto the street – to find herself totally helpless as thirty feet stumbled over her, two at a time.

A brief moment of total blackness followed, then bright lights – a hospital emergency room. Next she found herself on a hard bed, her wrists strapped down. A group of young doctors were standing around the bed. She heard a gray-haired doctor say, "We'll give her seventy-two hours. If there aren't any distinct improvements, we'll bring her in for exploratory brain surgery."

Marieji snapped her fingers. "Diana, wake now…and remember."

Diana's eyelids popped open. *Gaia. The jungle.*

"Speak your dreams," Marieji commanded.

Diana felt oddly disconnected. She began to recount her dream as though watching a movie, but her face stretched tight as she repeated the older doctor's words. "Oh no. How long have I been here? I need to wake up and–"

"You are fully awake," Marieji said. "This isn't a dream."

A ragged breath rasped up from out of her lungs. Diana raised a hand and explored the painful lump on the back of her head. "But what does it all mean? Seventy-two hours? And that dragon? It all seems so real, but…"

"It's as real as all this." Marieji swept her arm in a full circle. She watched Diana quietly, waiting for a response.

Diana turned from Marieji's intense gaze. *This is all just too much.*

The older woman's silence made her feel vulnerable, even more uncertain. She struggled to understand why they had brought her here. Who "they" were…what they really wanted from her. *Or maybe she's telling me the truth. Too strange,* she thought. *But one thing's for sure – I definitely have to get out of here.*

Marieji cleared her throat. "You have a choice to make,

Diana."

Here it comes, she choked. She remembered that tone of voice from childhood. That *"This is for your own good, whether or not you like it'"* tone of voice. Her uneasy feeling of vulnerability grew even stronger. "Choice?" Diana asked softly, "between what and what?"

"As I said yesterday, you have very little time to refocus back into your Earth body. We now know surgeons are about to cut open your skull, Diana. And I truly doubt your body can survive. I don't–"

"Survive? What do you mean?" Diana tried to blink away the intense, throbbing pain that smashed against the back of her head. "Are you telling me what I just dreamed is really real? What are you, some kind of psychic or something? Or is this a threat?"

Marieji pulled in a deep breath and exhaled slowly. "Diana. If your life ends on Earth, it also ends here."

She forced herself to concentrate on the older woman's eyes. She didn't want to believe her. How could she believe her? There had to be a reason, some explanation. She had to find a way to escape. *Maybe if I call her out,* she thought.

"Well then," Diana said coldly. "If you know so much about all this and really do want to help me, why don't you just let me go? Send me back home."

"If I did you would still be trapped in an almost lifeless coma."

Diana played the woman's words back in her mind. *Lifeless coma?* She had to somehow get to the truth. Her attention was drawn to the dragon's head medallion around

Marieji's neck. A brief vision of the fire-breathing dragon she had just seen in her dream drifted through the back of her mind, fueling her agitation.

"Wait a minute." Diana looked hard into Marieji's eyes. "Did you say that wasn't just a dream?"

"That is exactly what I'm trying to tell you, Diana. That wasn't a dream. It was a clear vision of your reality. And even if I could send you back, you'd still be in the coma. You have two choices."

"Choices? Between what and what?"

"You can live out your limited time here on Gaia, or you can step onto the warrior's path – prepare to face the dragon and try to pass back through the gate between our worlds."

The power of the woman's words seemed undeniable. Diana looked away. This shouldn't be happening. Couldn't be, but was. The heat of the sun suddenly felt oppressive. *She left out one option*, she thought. *If I can remember how I got here, I can just go back the same way. Just like that little bug that crawled back through the hole in the onion skin. I need to play along – until I figure out how to escape.*

Marieji sat silently looking at nothing in particular. "You must make a clear decision, Diana," she said softly. "You have limited time."

Diana chewed on her lip. She would definitely play along until she could make her bid for freedom, but decided to test the other's woman's intentions. "OK. If you won't send me back, then just show me where that gate is and I'll go back myself."

"To pass through the dragon's gate you must be able to

totally focus your consciousness in the present moment. Can you do that?" Marieji asked.

"Sure. Just show me that gate, or whatever it is, and I'm out of here."

Marieji lifted lightly to her feet. "Shall we test your ability to focus in the present moment, Diana?"

"Why not."

Marieji stared at Diana.

Diana silently returned her stare.

"Up!" Marieji suddenly commanded.

Diana scrambled to her feet as though her body had reacted to the command on its own.

Marieji pointed to a large black rock out in the middle of the river. Deep water swirled around both sides of the slick giant. "Step from those smaller rocks out onto that large black boulder there in the middle of the river."

She's got to be kidding, Diana thought. *Why would she—*

"Diana," Marieji insisted. "You said you can focus totally in the present moment. Show me."

Diana stepped cautiously from one rock to another until she finally managed to climb up onto the slick giant. The river rushed angrily around both sides, shooting a thick cloud of spray higher than her head. She hunkered down and shielded her eyes from the spray. Danger scratched at the back of her mind like a cat sharpening its claws on sandpaper. She looked over at Marieji for a sign.

"Come to your feet," Marieji shouted above the roar of the waterfall.

Stand up? Is she kidding. But if that will get me out of here, Diana thought, *I'll just go along with her.* She gulped, rose carefully to her feet, and threw her arms out to balance herself.

"Pay attention." Marieji shouted. "Hold your focus fully in the now. Let me tell you about the dragon's gate."

At the word "dragon" a brief vision of the fire-spitting beast from her dream burst into Diana's mind. She gasped, then ducked involuntarily when an imaginary fireball suddenly flew at her from out of nowhere.

She tumbled off the rock and into the water. The current immediately smashed her back against a rock, then pushed her beneath the surface and into a powerful whirlpool.

Diana opened her eyes, but saw nothing but swirling water. She felt herself loosing the will to fight, and remembered another time – what had she been – seven years old? The family was at the beach. A rip tide had jerked her feet from beneath her... dragged her across the ocean floor, then dumped her in deep water far out beyond the breakers. No one had seen it happen and...

Then there was the time when the canoe tipped over in the middle of the lake. Her parents had gone to town for groceries. *I wasn't supposed to take the canoe out alone. Not supposed to, but–*

A sudden sharp pain in her knee startled her into action. She seized at the trunk of a fallen tree, fought the current, and desperately dragged herself along the trunk to the safety of the river bank. She pulled herself up onto the dry ground, fell onto her knees, and heaved up river water.

She looked up to find Marieji standing over her, hands on hips.

"OK," Marieji said quietly. "Back up. You dropped your focus. This time pay attention."

"Pay attention. Are you kidding?" Diana gasped. *She's trying to kill me. This is no game.*

"Up! To pass through the gate you must be able to totally focus in the moment. Not off in past memories or future fantasies. You said you can do this. Show me, and I'll send you to the dragon's gate today."

Diana's anger slapped her fear away. She ignored the blood streaming down her leg from a deep gash in her knee and struggled back onto the slippery rock. *This is really crazy,* she thought, *but if this is all I have to do, then–*

"Pay attention," Marieji boomed.

"Hey," Diana shouted back. "I could get killed."

"Focus in the now," Marieji roared above the sound of the river. "You have less than seventy-two Earth hours. You must discover your true inner power, then face the dragon to return."

"What is the…" Diana's rage choked her.

"Be here now. Picture yourself facing the dragon."

At the word "dragon," Diana again tumbled off the rock into the angry water.

After Diana's fourth unsuccessful attempt to stay on the boulder, Marieji ordered to sit in front of her.

Diana settled onto the sand and wrapped her arms around her legs. A steady stream of blood sliced down her left leg like a red ribbon. She felt nearly blind from the throbbing headache and the water in her eyes.

What in God's name is this all about, she asked herself. *This woman definitely tried to kill me.*

"So, do you still feel you're capable of totally focusing in the moment?"

Diana failed to find a suitable reply. *I need to get out of here,* she thought. *She's going to kill me. I've got to find a way out of this.*

"Diana?"

"OK. Where am I failing?"

Marieji nodded and stood up. "You must learn to create your life in full consciousness in the present moment. Come." She held out a hand to Diana.

Diana gulped against the hard lump that had formed in her throat and took Marieji's hand. She would play along until she could find a way to escape, then find the gate by herself.

Marieji's gaze bore into her. "You face three challenges to prepare yourself to pass through the gate, Diana. There is no other way. You must learn to stand totally present in the moment. You must also overcome your limited ego self – to escape the grip of your fear, and look into the true nature of life. And then you must learn to consciously create your own reality. Do you understand?"

Of course I don't, Diana raged silently. *What a bunch of bull crap and–*

"To do this you must step onto the warrior's path – become one upon whom nothing is wasted."

* * * * *

"This can't be happening," Diana muttered as she limped along behind Marieji on the path to the village. She winced as she followed the older woman over a fallen tree and the tenuous scab on her left knee split open. Her fingers curled, uncurled, and curled again so tight that her knuckles turned white.

She remembered her visit to the jungle in Costa Rica the summer after high school graduation. It had been nothing like this. They had stayed in a four star resort with a swimming pool and a great dance floor. She wished she could just wake up and be home. *There's no waking up*, she reminded herself. *This is not a dream. Gaia, not Earth – a different skin of the same onion.* She struggled to make sense of what was happening to her, then her mind overloaded and shut down.

Marieji cleared her throat.

Diana shook herself. *Pay attention,* she reminded herself. She forced herself to focus on finding an escape route.

* * * * *

Diana followed Marieji into the outer fringes of the village, then through a cluster of about fifty huts. A network of well-worn paths led to other groups of huts barely visible through the thick foliage. A thin finger of blue-gray smoke curled up from what looked like a community fire pit.

A rag-tag band of young children hooted with joy and ran by in pursuit of an older girl spinning a wind whistle.

Several villagers greeted Marieji, eyeing Diana curiously.

A sharp turn in the path brought them to a large hand-hewed log building with a plank roof. Three men dressed in sand colored knee-length robes and high boots stood in front of the building. A fourth man dressed in tan shorts and a tunic stood with them talking excitedly.

Diana noted that one of the men held a rope connected to a string of heavily-loaded pack horses, and three saddle horses were tied to the porch rail.

"They're traders from across the Eastern badlands," Marieji explained. "They bring us our swords, knives and cooking pots. They bargain hard and long. Let's go see the stables and the garden. We'll get you some supplies on our way back."

"Eastern badlands?" Diana's eyes were drawn to the deeply worn horse trail leading from the building out into the jungle. It was clearly marked with fresh horse droppings. She dropped her eyes when Marieji turned to her.

She was certain she'd found her escape route, and didn't want to give her plan away.

CHAPTER SIX

*The path to awareness is complex,
a forced battle in which the unknown spurs you on.*

—*Arnold Mindell*

DIANA SNATCHED UP the net bag and dumped her dirty clothes onto the floor. She grabbed the fruit basket, stuffed the fruit into the bag, added a loaf of bread left over from dinner, then headed for the door. On an impulse, she turned back and pulled the cover off the bed, threw it over her shoulders, and stepped out onto the porch.

The sky was lit by a nearly full moon.

The hair on the back of her neck prickled as she stepped off the porch onto the path leading to the central village. The embers from the community campfire were still visible. *I can find the store from the fire pit,* she thought. *Just one step at a time, and I'll be fine.*

She set out alone in the moonlight.

The unmistakable taste of fear was thick in her mouth.

Diana froze just short of the central clearing. A single man stood at the fire pit poking at the coals with a long stick. *Can I circle around the clearing?* she asked herself. She decided not to chance being seen or heard, clenched her teeth, and hunched down with her back to a tree to wait.

* * * * *

The sky had begun to lighten when the solitary figure finally retired. Diana crept from the edge of the clearing and edged her way toward the community store. The neat row of canvas water bags still hung from the porch rail, exactly where she had seen them the day before.

She inched up to the porch and untied a bag, then crept silently to the small stream just behind the store. One cautious step at a time then brought her to the deeply worn horse trail. The droppings from the traders' horses were still fresh.

* * * * *

Diana stood at the edge of the jungle and peered out over the badlands in the first traces of early morning light. She felt a fierce exhilaration. No one could stop her now.

I can do it. She laughed aloud and strode from the jungle out onto the clear path left by the traders' horses. *They've got to know the way to the gate,* she told herself.

She spotted the smoke of a campfire just a short distance away and forced herself into a trot.

The sun was just rising above the eastern mountains as Diana reached the fire she'd seen from the edge of the jungle. She dropped the net bag and stood silently. There in the center of a tire-sized mound was a miniature volcano spewing a steady stream of red lava.

What she had thought was the traders' campfire was actually the crucible of a birthing volcano.

She looked around for the horse trail, but found no evidence of hoof prints in the rocky soil. Tears gathered. Diana brushed them away impatiently. She felt like a caged animal who had broken free, just to find itself in even greater danger.

* * * * *

Marieji pulled aside the door net and stepped into the hut. Had the young woman gone to the river to bathe? Her rapid visual sweep of the interior of the hut revealed that something was wrong. The bed cover was gone, as was the net bag – the soiled clothing from the bag thrown in a pile on the floor. The basket of fruit was empty. The towel hung on its peg, dry.

* * * * *

The wind began as a gentle wisp from the west – just enough to move the tops of the dry brush weed. Fine tendrils of yellow dust began to drift across the plateau, leaving behind miniature mounds of wind-sculpted sand.

Diana had searched for over two hours for a sign of hoof prints. Her mouth was dry with anxiety. She yearned for the river, the dark jungle, the village. *Pay attention*, she reminded herself. She took a drink, then bent down to examine the faint traces of what looked like an animal path.

Suddenly the quality of the light shifted. She stopped and studied the angle of the sun. Her head hurt, the wound on her knee had broken open, her feet ached. And the day had hardly begun.

It's OK, she reassured herself. *It's still early enough to go back. I can always –*

Without warning, a wind devil dropped a biting cloud of dust around her. Angry particles of sand slashed against her skin, stung her eyes. An enormous flock of birds flew overhead just behind the swirling funnel – obviously fleeing something even worse.

Diana spun around and gasped at the source of the birds' panic. An angry cloud had eaten the entire western horizon and was boiling across the badlands directly at her.

Got to take cover! Her instincts took over. She ripped the bed cover from her shoulders, wrapped it around herself, and dove behind a large rock.

* * * * *

Marieji settled down onto the porch of the hut to analyze what she had discovered. The young woman, Diana, had obviously bolted. Run off. She didn't have the skills to survive very long. Where would she most likely go? Off into the jungle? No. It was clear she was deeply afraid of the jungle. So where would she go?

She suddenly recalled Diana's interest in the traders – her questions about where they camped at night. *Could she have followed them out onto the badlands? That could prove even more dangerous than the jungle. And if she actually managed to catch up with them, they would probably…*

Marieji leapt up and set out in a determined gait toward the central village.

* * * * *

The storm was hypnotic, endless. Time stretched out to infinity as the acrid sand and wind rushed around the rock. Diana struggled with the anxiety threatening to overwhelm her. She had escaped, after all. She would find the traders' trail once the storm was over.

But exhaustion began to wear at her. In a vision she saw herself back on Earth about eight years old – the family was vacationing in the little seaside town of Santa Cruz. The sky was clear blue – the color of her Mother's favorite cobalt glass vase. She was on the beach. Warm, tawny yellow sand stretched as far as she could see. The sun on her body…the sound of the waves–

The danger of her situation interrupted her memories. *I might very well die out here,* she realized.

Her mind began to spin through yet another waking dream.

She began to recall the times death had touched her life. Her dog, Bones. She wept to rememberl the look in his eyes when he fell at her feet after being hit by a car. She was only ten, and he was her best friend in the world. He died in her arms.

Then she revisited the gut-wrenching suicide of Janie, one of her closest friends. Of seeing her hooked up to a machine that pumped air into her lungs. But Janie was clearly not there.

What is death? She reflected on the death of her vision of herself as an artist. Her childlike trust of her natural talent had imploded, just died, when her submission to her high school art show was judged inappropriate. Even more traumatic had been the gradual, mind-numbing death of her marriage. And now, GreenWatch's prediction of the highly probable death of life on Earth. Earth. Would she ever see it again?

With a start, Diana realized that the howling wind had been replaced by an eerie silence. She sat up and pulled the cover from her head. The daylight had disappeared into a seamless brown nothingness. The sun was a dull orange globe – motionless and vacant. The sky was the same grainy brown as the dusty badlands.

Diana considered her goal of finding the traders' trail and realized the hopelessness of her search. *I better just return to the jungle,* she thought. She stood and turned in a full circle, then stiffened. The entire landscape had changed – become totally featureless in the heavy dust.

* * * * *

Marieji swung her leg over the horse's flanks and settled easily into the saddle. She turned to scan her companions, then lifted her chin toward the lean, straight-backed man seated lightly on the dappled stallion to her right. "Barjo knows the badlands best. He's in charge of the search team. She can't have gone too far. But we have no idea which direction she set out in…or even if she's still alive."

Barjo signaled for a stop just beyond the edge of the jungle, stood in the stirrups, and looked out over the badlands. "There's been a heavy dust storm, so we'll just have to do the best we can. Marieji, you take three and fan out to the west. Corsa, you take south. Let's meet at the stable by sundown. No sense trying to search at night."

He nodded to the three riders closest to him. "You three come with me to the east.." He settled back down into the saddle and reined his horse toward the east. "That dumb Earthie is probably already dead anyway," he mumbled.

* * * * *

Thirst tore at her throat. Diana wiped her parched lips with the back of her hand and her lower lip split open. *I need water…water.*

She remembered dropping the net bag containing her food and water when she dove behind the rock for shelter. *Where did it go?* she asked herself. It took only a short search for her to realize that it was hopeless. The wind had obviously carried the bag away, or buried it under a mound of sand. She would have to make do.

She leaned against the rock that had sheltered her from the storm and stared out over the dull brown landscape. Her eyes stung; she rubbed at them impatiently. Suddenly a huge lizard scrambled out from beneath the rock and raced across the sand. *Lucky,* she thought. *It knows exactly where it's going.*

That's it, she realized. *I have to get back to the jungle while it's still light.* She turned to face the sun. *That must be west. So the jungle must be to the right.* She looked for a sign of trees, but saw only the same featureless, dust-colored horizon.

Diana had wandered for hours, increasingly anxious when she suddenly realized that the bottom of the orange-red sun was dropping behind a mountain range. She stumbled and knew she had to stop. It was getting dark and she was out in the middle of the badlands, without any hope of finding her way to the jungle in the darkness. *Are there wild creatures out here?* She sucked in a sharp breath between tightly clenched teeth. *Is there any doubt?*

As the final tip of the sun disappeared, she wrapped herself in the bed cover and curled into a desperately tight ball against a small mound of rocks and sand. Her steadily mounting fear totally overrode her desperate need for sleep.

* * * * *

Barjo and Corsa turned their horses loose in the corral, then added their saddles and bridles to the neat row along the corral fence.

Barjo hooked his bridle over the saddle horn and leaned against the fence. "Think there's any hope for her, Corsa?"

Corsa shook her head. "Doubt it. Even if she gets through the night, the sun will be out full force tomorrow morning. And if she did by chance manage to catch up with those traders, for sure we'll never see her again."

"Think so?"

"Come on, Barjo. Those men are out in those badlands for months at a time. Think they're going to waste time bringing a wandering woman back to the jungle? They'll just lay claim to her. Have you forgotten what happened to Martee's girl?"

* * * * *

Diana opened her eyes to a clear mid-morning sky. The sun was hot, right through the bed cover. Too hot. Her first thought was of water. Food didn't matter any more.

Her desperate need for water brought her to her feet.

She steadied herself against a rock, shielded her eyes and scanned the horizon. No jungle. Suddenly she tilted her head. *Is that a pond? Trees? Yes!*

She wrapped the bed cover over her head and shoulders as a sun shield and began to walk as fast as she could. *The jungle can wait,* she reasoned. *I need water.*

* * * * *

Barjo shielded his eyes and scanned the badlands. "We'll search until mid-day, then that's it. If she is out here alone, she'll never survive the sun. No sense putting the horses out in this heat for nothing." He reined his horse toward the eastern horizon. "Let's go. We'll use the same teams as yesterday."

* * * * *

The sun was mid-heaven when Diana finally stopped walking. Ponds, lakes, even oceans of water surrounded her in every direction.

She rasped a deep sigh. She was tired – very tired – and had chased one mirage after another all morning. She pulled the bed cover closer over her head and closed her eyes to rest them. Hunger had turned from pain to a dull ache; but thirst had become an obsession. She had to have water.

Need to rest first.

She slid to her haunches by a rock.

Wait, an inner voice insisted. *Maybe the traders will come by while I'm resting. I need a signal.* Sharp pain stabbed through her head. She reached up to rub the back of her neck. *The bandage. I can make a flag.*

Diana staggered over to a spindly bush and snapped off a long leafless arm. She pulled the bandage from her head, ripped it down the middle lengthwise, then tied the largest piece to the end of the limb.

She braced her makeshift flag on top of the rock with a pile of stones, then wrapped the rest of the cloth around the greenish, oozing cut on her knee. Finally she anchored one edge of the bed cover to the top of the rock, secured the lower edge with a few small rocks, and crawled under her crude shelter to rest.

As she slipped into exhaustion, her past began to turn

before her in vignettes. What had she accomplished that had given any true meaning to her life? She reflected, and came to the realization that she had never truly, passionately committed herself to anything. Her life had been a series of lukewarm efforts toward success in many scattered ventures. But each time she had stopped short of total passionate commitment – even with her art. She had just stopped short and quit.

Was I afraid to discover I wasn't as good as I thought? Was it better not to find out? Was that it? Was it fear of failure? Had it been easier to quit? Or was it...

* * * * *

Barjo reined in his horse scanned the horizon. The other three riders watched and waited. "It's mid-day," he finally announced flatly. "That's it."

The young man to Barjo's right hooked his leg over the saddle horn, untied a canteen from the back of his saddle, and lifted it to his lips. He suddenly jerked the canteen from his mouth. "Barjo, look."

"What? Where?"

"Look." He pointed to an outcropping of rocks. "Over there. It's a flag and...is that a tent?"

"Probably traders."

"No. I don't see any horses."

"Look. Over by that large group of rocks. Over there. Don't you see it?"

"Oh yeah, I do." Bargo nodded his head. "Probably has his horse on the other side of that large rock formation."

"Barjo, I've got a feeling that–"

"Look, the sun is mid-sky. We need to get the horses out of this heat."

"It's not that far, Barjo."

Barjo's face clouded over. *The sun is too hot to mess with, but it does look like only one tent. Do the traders ever travel alone? Never*, he admitted. "OK. We'll check it out, but we're done after that. Agreed?"

In her dream Diana heard horses. *The traders?* Someone shouted something about a flag. *A flag?* She wondered at that. *Is there a flag? Are those really voices? Or am I just dreaming again?*

The sudden splash of cold water on her face startled her to awareness. She opened sand-scratched eyes to the sight of four faces bending over her. *The traders? No.* She recognized one – the lean man she had seen at the stable. The villagers had come for her. She reached out to grasp the canteen of the man who had splashed the water on her face.

CHAPTER SEVEN

*Setting goals is the first step in turning the invisible into
the visible – the foundation for all success in life.*

—*Anthony Robbins*

DIANA SAT ON the edge of the bed, a clean bandage on her
head, her body working hard to recover from severe
dehydration and exposure. She dropped her eyes when Marieji
entered the hut with a tray of food.

The older woman gently placed the tray on the bed, pulled
up the stool, and sat down silently.

It was a painful silence.

Diana stared at the back of her hands, but could feel the
other woman's eyes burning into her. She exhaled deeply and
tried to keep her mind blank, waiting for what she knew was
probably coming.

"Diana, it's amazing we found you out there in the
badlands. You would have been dead by now. Is that what

you wanted to do, Diana? Did you want to die out there?"

Diana struggled to organize her thoughts. She had thought she could escape. Would they ever trust her again? Was she in even more danger now? "How...how can you even ask me that?" she stammered.

Marieji pulled a knife from her belt sheath, sliced several pieces off a yellow cheese, then arranged them between two slices of bread. She held out the sandwich to Diana. "Eat."

Diana accepted the cheese and bread, then stared at it vacantly. Fear burned in her chest. Her hope to escape had been totally crushed. *Maybe I should just take a chance. Just ask her to send me back through the gate. But she said I'd still be in a coma. What if I can't pull out of the coma?*

"Diana? Do you want to die?"

She groped in her mind for an answer. *Do I want to die? Of course not.* Tears swelled to her eyes. She couldn't live out the rest of her life in a coma. Neither could she just sit waiting in this jungle until her life, or her brain, came to an ugly end at the hands of those surgeons. *Not acceptable.* And it was now clear that there was no way to run – no way to escape. She'd have to tough it out somehow.

"Marieji," Diana sighed. "Of course I want to live. How can you even ask me that? I only hope that–"

Marieji shook her head. "Hope won't get you anywhere, Diana. You need to master your own sense of being and go through some dramatic changes. This won't be easy. You can't afford to play any more games with yourself– to fall into denial or pretend this isn't happening."

She wiped the blade of her knife and slid it back into the

sheath. "I'm willing to help you, Diana. But for now, your body needs food. Eat."

Diana lifted the sandwich, pushed past the pain of her split lower lip and took a bite.

* * * * *

Marieji hummed quietly to herself and studied the young woman as she devoured the food. *Can I successfully prepare this one for her moment of truth in the small amount of time available? Possible, but not too likely.* She recalled the last woman who had fallen through the dragon's gate and tried to return. She hadn't made it to the gate. Fear had driven her to take refuge in the caves, and she was most likely still there – hiding from the very thing that could set her free.

* * * * *

Diana finished the last of the tea and looked up at Marieji. She felt embarrassed, vulnerable, stupid. It was clear that the other woman could see right through her. Obviously the best thing to do was accept any offer of help. "OK. What do I need to do?"

Marieji shifted her weight on the stool and looked directly into Diana's eyes. "The seeds of your solution are already within you. We only need to cultivate them – to grow you into a warrior."

"A warrior?" Diana sputtered. "Look Marieji, I have to tell you that I'm...I'm just a graphic designer. I've never really been a serious athlete. I mean, I've jogged a little, but never–"

"Diana, it's OK to feel uncertain. But in truth, you probably spent years preparing for that coma – preparing to face the dragon."

"Hey. I certainly never meant to end up in a coma."

"That may not be entirely true. From what you've told me, you were feeling almost totally overwhelmed by life. Isn't that true?"

She shook her head. *That's a reality,* Diana admitted to herself. *Overwhelmed is an understatement.* "That's true," she said quietly.

"So, your coma was probably an unconscious place of safety. In many ways, what you did is no different from what many people in your time are doing, Diana. Many of the most sensitive, spiritual-minded people on Earth today are actually sleepwalking."

"Sleepwalking?"

"Yes. They know very well that both their environment and their society are collapsing around them. But they feel helpless to do anything about it, so they try to protect their sanity by closing their eyes to what's happening."

A mental picture of the recent riot in South Central LA flooded into Diana's mind. The TV cameras had followed the rioting blow by blow. She recalled the vacant looks on the faces of many who were interviewed – their obvious sense of helpless despair. *What she said was true, but what could they do?* "Hey, Marieji. Try to be fair. It's just too overwhelming. I mean–"

Marieji rose to her feet, crossed her arms and stood

quietly. "Diana, I'll bet you felt the early signs of a deep consciousness shift long before you came here – discontent, restlessness, and most certainly despair. What you were feeling was actually a wake-up call. In a desperate move, a higher part of your self finally just took over – dumped you right into that coma and through the dragon's gate. You could say your higher self tried to shock you into a more conscious state of being. You're fortunate."

"Fortunate?" Diana sputtered. "Are you kidding?"

"I'm serious," Marieji smiled. "Many spend their entire lives standing on the brink – the very edge – of great personal transformation. But few actually take the great leap into the arms of their passion."

Diana reached up and touched the hard lump on the back of her head. She compared herself to the mental state Marieji had described. She had to admit there was some truth to what she had said. "You really think that's true, don't you?"

"I know it to be true, Diana. A powerful new race of spiritually adept warriors is awakening today on Earth from out of the turmoil of your day. Their higher selves are throwing them into great personal crises to wake them up. Loss of jobs, major financial crises, interpersonal catastrophes – wake-up calls appear in many forms. They are being called upon to turn from despair and empower themselves – to unleash their passion and create powerful new meaning in their lives."

"Passion?"

"Yes, passion is the fuel for the moment of truth – the moment in which you choose to create true meaning in your life. But most of those destined to become warriors first feel a deep longing within themselves – a sense of almost starving on a cellular level for some sense of meaning. Real meaning. Something to believe in so passionately it rages like a forest fire in the pit of their stomachs."

"I've felt something like that, Marieji. I've always wanted to have hope, but…"

"But?"

"But how can I find hope? I've been trapped in some kind of madness. It seems as though my whole life has fallen into a black hole – some kind of deadening chaos. Nothing makes sense any more."

"Diana, hope isn't something you find. It's created. This is what marks the difference between a warrior and an innocent. A warrior takes hold of the energy of their despair, turns it into a positive expression of hope, then fuels their action with passion. Passionate action burns despair to a cinder, creates entirely new possibilities."

Diana admitted she hadn't thought of her own life in quite that way. The older woman's words were compelling, even exciting. She straightened her back and leaned forward. "So what do I need to do, Marieji?"

"You need to be willing to tolerate some chaos for a while – as you strengthen your trust in your intuitive wisdom. And you need to spark that passionate burning within yourself. Do you have a passion to live?"

A passion to live? Diana breathed out a deep sigh, shook her head. "For sure I don't want to – die."

Marieji bent over and gently lifted Diana's chin until they were eye to eye. "Then we'll start with that, and fan it into a passion if we can. You can only succeed if you learn to allow your passion to consume you, then let new possibilities materialize in your life."

"Marieji. I'm still afraid that–"

Marieji straightened up, stepped back and held her hand up for silence. "Rest now. I'll come early in the morning for you. Tomorrow you step onto the warrior's path – begin to move past your fear."

Diana watched silently as the older woman parted the door net and stepped out into the twilight. *Move past my fear?* She blew out her breath. *We'll see. She really has no idea just how deep that fear goes right now.*

CBEO

CHAPTER EIGHT

The ability of the mind to extend its influence
seems limitless…even when impossible
obstacles confront it.

— *Deepak Chopra, MD*

DOCTOR KATIE WHITE, first year medical resident at LA's
New Community Hospital, wiped an afternoon of coffee stains
from the cafeteria table with a paper napkin. Oblivious to her
surroundings, she dropped a computer printout on the table and
pulled a battered pack of Earl Grey tea from her pocket. She
separated the bag from its yellow flap and slid it into a cup of
steaming water.

White nibbled at the muffin-of-the-day, but shook her head
to find that "fresh strawberry" referred only to a spoonful of
seedy jam in the middle of the bone-dry muffin. She looked at
the muffin in disgust, dropped it back on the plate and pushed
the it aside. She unfolded the computer printout and pulled a

red felt tip pen from the breast pocket of her white coat. She tapped the pen end over end as she scanned the tracings.

A crewcut man clad in the hospital's green ER scrubs walked up to the table, waited impatiently to get her attention. "Join you?" he finally asked.

White glanced up, nodded. "Of course. Sit."

He grimaced at his first swallow of the bitter coffee. "What's that?" He pointed at the printout.

"The baseline brainwave readings for a comatose Jane Doe. The one in IC. You guys admitted her just a few hours ago."

"Oh yeah. I hear you've hooked her up to a room full of fancy EEG hardware. How'd you get that past our famed Chief of Surgery, Charles 'the Bear' Brennan?"

White shook her head. "The Bear himself gave permission. I'm also studying two other female comatose patients. They're long-term though."

"What're you looking for?"

"I've got a hunch that some comatose people are actually in altered states. Just a theory at this point."

He pulled a candy bar from his pocket, tore off the outer package, meticulously opened the thin inner foil wrapping and smoothed it out, then separated the bar into pieces and positioned it on the foil. "Like some Swiss chocolate? So you think brainwaves will prove your point?"

"Maybe. I saw some possible evidence years ago, on a trip to Brazil – Christmas vacation in my high school senior year."

"Oh?"

"Our teacher took us to meet a shaman and walk on fire.

It was quite an experience."

"Yeow. So did you actually walk on fire?"

"Sure did. Did you know those coals are 1200 degrees Fahrenheit?"

"Gads. Did you burn your feet?"

"No. Funny. None of us did. First time I went across a coal actually stuck to the side of my foot. But I just brushed it off when I got to the other side. My foot wasn't burned at all."

"How could that be?"

"Logically, I don't know. It has to be the power of the mind. Anyway, I have the feeling that such states of being can actually be measured."

He tapped the tracings. "So how does this fit in?"

"Let me finish my story. Our teacher brought a lady friend with him – a UC Berkeley PhD candidate. Her name was Jane, Jane…something"

"And?"

"She had this battery-operated brainwave measuring device with her, and hooked the shaman up to it before and after the ceremony."

"You're kidding. Out there in the jungle?"

"Yep."

"Well. What did she–"

"Hey, slow down," White laughed. "I've only got five minutes of my break left. But I'll tell you this much, his brainwaves were real different from mine."

"She measured yours?"

"She had to. I followed her around like a puppy." White folded up the computer printout and shoved it into the back of her clipboard. "Tell you what. Since you're so interested, I'll be happy to tell you more. But not now–"

"So, when?"

"I'm only scheduled for half a day, morning hours, on Thursday. Meet me here about two?"

"You're on."

* * * * *

The curly-headed nurse tapped the IV tube, then gazed quietly at Diana's comatose body. "Let's see. Six hours since admission. You seem calm enough now. Like to unstrap those wrist restraints." She shook her head. "But the order is here on your chart."

୧୫୨୦

CHAPTER NINE

All any of us have to do is suspend our doubts
and distractions just long enough…

—*James Redfield*

DIANA WOKE AND knew where she was.

Not Earth. Gaia.

Her fingers explored her swollen left knee. *No way to pretend this is a dream,* she admitted. *Hurts bad.*

She didn't want to think about being on Gaia. *Maybe if I go back to sleep…*

She took three slow breaths to smooth out the ripple of anxiety creeping around the back of her mind, wrapped her right arm around her torso, then closed her eyes and tried to will herself back to sleep.

A distinct sound interrupted her attempt. Someone, or something, was out on the porch. Diana poked her little finger cautiously into her right ear, still ringing from heavy doses of river water several days before, then propped herself up on her elbow. "Oh no," she moaned. "It's her again."

"Looking for breakfast?" Marieji asked Chat Chew, who gazed with feline intensity at the thick underbrush at the edge of the jungle.

"Mee...ep."

"First go wake your friend Diana, Chat Chew. Tell her it's time to leave the comfort of her bed."

"Mee...ep." The cat turned her attention to the low moan that had come from the hut.

"Come, join us," Marieji called.

"The nightmare continues," Diana muttered. She ran her fingertips lightly over the rough scab on her knee and tried to straighten her leg. She discovered pain – left hip all the way down into her ankle and foot. No – her entire body was at odds with itself. She pushed herself upright on the bed, then braced her back against a support pole running from the floor to the ceiling of the hut.

Diana's stiff muscles resisted even the smallest movement. She got her clothes from the table, then sat down gingerly on the edge of the bed to dress. *Gads*, she thought. *Feels like someone beat on me with an iron pipe.*

She shuffled outside stiff-legged.

"Sit and eat," Marieji patted the porch boards.

Diana shoved her left leg out in front of her to avoid bending the knee, then eased down onto the porch.

Marieji held out a red fruit and a small loaf of freshly baked bread. "So how do you feel today?" she smiled.

Diana stared silently at her bruised knee. *Beat up*, she thought. *Looks like I really did it to myself.*

"Indeed you did."

Diana's back snapped upright. Had she spoken her thoughts aloud? *No.* "Did you just read my mind?"

Marieji laughed deeply.

Something really weird about her, Diana thought. *In one way I really trust her, all the way down into myself. But on the other hand...* "Do you do anything other than play mind games?" Diana snapped. "If you hadn't done that to me at the river, maybe I..."

Marieji silently returned her look, then shrugged. "Diana, the only game we're playing is called waking you up. No one is doing anything to you. You're doing it all to yourself."

Diana cradled her left knee in both hands, slowly bending her leg to ease the stiffness. "Oh, sure," she laughed coldly. "I'm doing it to myself."

"Are you ready to step onto the warrior's path?"

Prickly heat moved up Diana's neck and into her face. *I hate the feeling of vulnerability this woman gives me,* she thought. She stared into the jungle, feeling very lonely and uncertain. *But I've got to get control of myself.*

Marieji paused and watched Chat Chew leap into the air to catch a large beetle, then turned to Diana. "Are you paying attention, Diana? Your first challenge is to learn to truly focus your attention. The act of giving attention is what brings all things to you."

If she's just going to preach at me.

Marieji snapped her fingers in Diana's face. "Wake up,"

she laughed. "Everything in your life happens because of where you put your attention. Be here now."

Diana spun to face her tormentor, her face burning with unbridled anger. Her knee hurt. Her whole body hurt. "Can't you just lay off for a while, Marieji? Let me work it out myself."

"Diana, you really don't have the luxury of time. You can either take control of your life – step onto the warrior's path – or remain a victim of your own fears and allow those surgeons to cut into your brain.

"OK, stop trying to belittle me. I'll give it a try."

Marieji laughed a deep resounding laugh and slapped her thighs with both hands. "It will take far more than a try. You must exercise full intent to stand as a warrior."

Diana snorted as an impossible image of herself in clumsy armor crowded into her mind. *Not good*, she thought. *Not good, not good, not good...*

"Are you angry, Diana?"

"No, I'm..." Diana struggled against the rising sense of anxiety and anger that had planted rocks in her stomach and throat. "Hey. I've got a right to be angry."

Marieji silently pointed at a huge bird that had swooped down on a small creature at the edge of the jungle. Diana cringed as the bird lifted up into the air, a tiny mouse clutched in its bright red talons.

"Fear plucks your power from you just as easily," Marieji said quietly. "Anger is a slight improvement. It's more powerful than feeling sorry for yourself. But it too just robs you of your power. Do you understand what I'm saying?"

Diana grabbed another piece of the fruit Marieji had placed on the porch. She jammed her teeth into the soft flesh. A stream of sticky red juice ran down her forearm and dripped off her elbow. It seemed as though her pain and fear meant nothing to the older woman. Nothing at all. She was treating her like a child – threatening her with stories of dragons and warriors. She roughly spat the seeds out onto the path.

"You must learn to look to the source of your anger, Diana. Anger is far too powerful to just spit out into the air. It's a weapon that can easily turn against you."

Diana snorted again, then angrily wiped her fruit-stained hands on her clean shorts.

"All right." Marieji chuckled and rose lightly to her feet. "It's time to step onto the warrior's path. Let's see if we can improve your ability to focus in the present moment."

Diana limped along behind Marieji on the well worn path leading to the central village.

* * * * *

Marieji greeted two women who walked by, then turned onto a narrow path leading to a small pond encircled with moss covered rocks.

Diana noticed that the pond was covered with a dense blanket of algae, and emptied at its far end into a muddy ditch. Her eyes were drawn to the odd structure hanging above the ditch. Long, leather-wrapped bamboo poles dangled from a tall frame. A narrow plank beneath the poles spanned the full length of the ditch.

"This is the place of our beginning," Marieji said, pointing to the pond.

"Beginning?"

"Yes. As I told you Diana, Gaia was born in your time – during the Great Change that began just before the end of the millennium. My ancestors were among those who turned from despair and sought positive alternatives. Many initially met in conferences, and finally left the cities to create little self-sustaining communities. Our village had just such a beginning, and this pond played an important part."

"So this was your water supply?"

"No," Marieji laughed. "We were fortunate to discover the value of what grows in the pond – the algae."

"That green slimy stuff?"

"That slime, as you call it, is the oldest food on Gaia, and also the oldest food on your Earth."

"So?"

"The algae is the basic food the Creative Force provided to sustain life as we know it – our basic cellular food." Marieji laughed at the Diana's look of disgust. "It's true, Diana. Eating the algae helped the early villagers transform on a cellular level – to become mentally, physically and spiritually clear enough to consciously pass through the vibrational gate between Earth and Gaia."

"They ate that pond scum? Yuck." Diana watched in disbelief as Marieji knelt down by the pond, cupped her hand and dipped it into the water.

She lifted out a palm full of glistening emerald green filaments that flowed through her fingers and back into the water. "Does this look like pond scum? Hardly. We'll get you a supply. You can discover the benefits for yourself."

"Ugh. Forget it."

Marieji laughed. "OK. Let's practice getting you focused in the now." She motioned for Diana to follow her to the odd apparatus at the far end of the pond.

A group of young children ran past, then stopped on the path to play a game of rock rolling.

"Watch this, Diana." Marieji took hold of a thick rope tied to the end of the hanging apparatus and gave it a jerk. The hanging poles began to swing back and forth across the plank. "The object is to walk over the length of the plank without being struck by a pole," she explained.

"No way. Impossible."

"Oh it's possible, all right. The secret is to totally focus your attention in the moment and just trust your natural instincts."

Diana was shocked at the weight of the pole as it struck her shoulder and threw her off the narrow plank. She landed on her side with a loud glop in the thick green mud. She sat up, to the delighted laughter of the children, dripping mud and burning with indignation.

On the next try she was knocked into the ditch trying to avoid the fourth pole. By now the children had stopped their game to watch her.

"Up you go," Marieji laughed.

Diana felt anger heat up her face beneath the mud, but was not about to let the older woman make a fool of her. "OK self," she hissed, "toughen up." She set her teeth, and choked back her anger and frustration.

"Toughen up?" Marieji chuckled. "This isn't a strength contest, Diana. Being tough won't get you anywhere. What you need to do is become flexible and playful – adopt the attitude of a child."

Diana ran her hands through her mud-caked hair and held them up in front of her, palms up. She laughed an angry laugh. "Oh sure. This is supposed to be fun?"

Marieji nodded her head silently, turned and called to the group of children. "Want to play? Come join us."

The first child made it across the plank on his third try, throwing his muddy arms into the air in a victory gesture. A girl scrambled to be next.

When all three of the children had managed to walk the full length of the plank, Marieji pointed to Diana. "Now it's her turn," she laughed.

"On no," Diana protested.

"The worst has already happened. You're a muddy mess. So why not just let go and try. Just trust yourself."

Only two poles to go, she thought. In that instant Diana understood what Marieji meant by focusing in the now. She heard the low whoosh of air, closed her eyes, and dove into the muddy ditch. The tip of the weighted pole slapped hard against her right heel.

* * * * *

Diana settled onto one of the logs circling the community fire pit. *I'm exhausted,* she thought. *How many times did it take me to cross that plank today? Twenty?*

The woman next to her glanced over, nodded, then turned back to the man she had been talking to. *About as friendly as a snake,* Diana thought. *I never thought I'd miss LA.* She picked up a twig and began to absently peel away the thin bark with her thumbnail.

Two scruffed black boots suddenly appeared directly in front of her. Diana looked up to an intense, deeply tanned woman – her hands shoved deep into the pockets of tight-fitting riding pants.

"Marieji tells me you're mine tomorrow Earthie," the woman smirked. She laughed a hollow laugh. "Hope you're real good with horses."

* * * * *

When Diana finally got to bed she knew she would never sleep. Old images crowded into her mind – again and again through the night she recalled being twelve years old and at Girl Scout summer camp. She was one of a small group of campers who were riding horseback – ambling along in a line behind a guide, laughing in a sunlit meadow.

Suddenly her horse was singled out by a huge swarm of bees. The horse screamed and ran off into the meadow, desperately whirling and bucking.

Diana clearly recalled flying through the air – the loud snap of her leg bone as she smashed against a rock. Her childhood love of horses had ended on that day – had been replaced by an undeniable, lifelong fear.

CHAPTER TEN

*When our souls are on fire, old beliefs and opinions
can be consumed. These times of inner burning have
been called the dark nights of the soul.*

—*Joan Borysenko, PhD*

DIANA RELUCTANTLY FOLLOWED Marieji into the pungent,
close darkness of the stable.

Horses. The nagging inner voice started up again. *Not
good…not good, not good…*

"Marieji?" A deep male voice called out from the
shadows.

Diana focused carefully on the muscular man that stepped
from a dark corner to greet them. *Great build*, she thought. The
tight brown pants and tall boots looked good on him. *Nice face.
Not Mel Gibson, but definitely a hunk.*

Marieji looked at Diana strangely, shook her head, then
turned to the man and hooked her thumb in Diana's direction.
"Barjo, would you please outfit this one for riding?"

"Huh," he snorted. "The Earthie we saved from the badlands."

Diana glared back defiantly.

Barjo shrugged and hitched up his belt, returned her gaze dispassionately, then calmly took her measure with his eyes.

Diana had just struggled into the tight-fitting pants and high black boots when she heard Marieji's voice. The scab on her left leg had split open. Hot, sticky blood had already seeped into the knee of the riding pants. *Won't give them the satisfaction of favoring my knee,* she promised herself.

"Diana?" Marieji called again.

Diana came around the corner and immediately recognized the woman standing next to Marieji – the same booted woman who had approached her the night before at the community fire.

"Here she is, Corsa." Marieji lifted her chin toward Diana.

Diana shuffled nervously in the unfamiliar boots and breeches, painfully aware of the rough cloth scraping against her knee. *She's definitely not too friendly,* she thought. She tried to match the other woman's direct gaze.

"Diana, this is Corsa. She is our finest horsewoman. She'll teach you to ride."

Diana set her teeth as the tall woman leaned against the stable wall, slowly looked her over head to foot, then shook her head. "I really do doubt it, Marieji," the horsewoman commented.

Diana sucked in her breath as Corsa stepped toward her, extended a tightly muscled arm, and poked a tanned finger into the soft layer of flab around her waist.

"Not so good, Marieji."

"Do what you can, Corsa," Marieji commented as she turned to leave. "She must be prepared to face the dragon."

Corsa slapped a hand to her forehead. "You? Face the dragon?" she moaned. "Do you have any idea what it would take to make you a warrior?" She shook her head sadly. "For sure you'll be my downfall. You truly will."

Diana stood silently. *Not good, not good, not good,* she thought. "Stop that," she muttered to herself.

"What'd you say?" Corsa barked.

"Nothing."

Corsa shook her head. "Come with me." She spun on her heel and strode toward the wide, sunlit doorway at the far end of the stable.

Diana followed her closely, then stumbled in the dim light when Corsa suddenly stopped to lift a braided rope halter from a peg near the stable door. *This really isn't going well,* Diana thought. *And now, horses!*

They stepped out of the stable into a sun-flooded, dusty corral area.

Corsa held the halter up in Diana's face. "Do you know what this is?"

Diana studied the deeply tanned face before her, and clearly recalled the face of the guide at Girl Scout camp when he looked down at her lying on the ground. He had been very angry. She winced at the memory.

"Can you talk?" Corsa asked roughly.

Diana nodded her head. "Yes. It's…it's for a horse."

"Oh very good," Corsa said in mock appreciation. "And I don't suppose you've ever been on a horse."

Diana shrugged, tried choked back her frustration, despair, and fear. She could see she was in serious trouble. This woman obviously had no compassion at all.

"Well. Have you?"

"A few times," Diana replied softly.

"Will you please speak up."

"A few times. A few times, as a child."

"OK, warrior," Corsa laughed dryly. "Put this halter on that little horsie over there with the two white stockings." She pointed out a large mare in one of the adjoining corrals. "Then come find me."

Diana took the halter from Corsa and limped over to the corral. She studied the mare standing quietly in the shade at the far side of the corral. Her head throbbed in the blistering sun. She remembered the swarm of bees, the way the horse had shrieked. *Got to stop that,* she thought. *I've got to get hold of myself.*

Diana steeled herself and slid awkwardly through the wooden rails. "Here horse," she called, moving one small step at a time toward the mare. The fact that the horse didn't seem to notice her made her even more nervous. She slowly moved closer and closer, never taking her eye off the mare.

When she was within a few feet, she cautiously reached out her hand in what she hoped the horse would see as a gesture of friendship. The mare suddenly looked right at her, snorted, and began to paw at the dust.

Diana fell back several steps and slid out through the fence rails to plan her strategy from safer ground. Again the mare paid no attention to her. It was obvious to Diana that a script for a tricky game between horse and woman was forming.

"Not going to be easy," she sighed.

* * * * *

Diana's face and clothes were deeply caked with sweat and dust by the time the sun was in the mid-morning sky. Time and time again she had approached the mare, but each time she tried to touch her had been worse. The horse had begun by biting at her, then progressed to rearing, and finally kicking.

Diana leaned against the fence. "How in blazes will I ever do this?" she fumed.

The mare snorted and pawed the earth.

She could feel the jungle heat getting to her. The buzz of the horse flies had grown steadily louder, and luminous blue spots were dancing around the periphery of her vision.

"OK," she sighed. "I'll give it one more try." She swatted at a horse fly that had lighted on her arm, gripped the halter in one sweaty hand, and crawled back through the corral rails.

The mare immediately dropped her ears, lowered her head, and began to paw at the dust with her right front hoof.

Diana pressed her back up against the corral fence and set her teeth. "OK horse," she took a tentative step forward. "Just give me a break, will you?"

The big bay snorted, reared, kicked her heels into the air, and began to spin in a series of tight, dusty circles. Then, entirely without warning, she raced out of the cloud of dust and headed right for Diana.

She threw herself down in the dirt and rolled wildly under the fence.

The mare tore by in a fit – leaving Diana sitting in the dust, eyes blazing with anger and frustration. She leapt to her feet, threw down the halter, and began to jump up and down on it furiously.

She was still stomping the halter into the dust when Marieji appeared from around the corner of the stable, a carrying bag slung over her shoulder.

"Diana?" Marieji called. "I have some lunch. Wash up and come join me."

She snarled at the halter one more time, then spun on her heel and stalked to the stream behind the stable. She threw cool water on her arms and face, then discovered a new problem – beneath the thick layer of sweat-caked dust was the beginning of a deep pink sunburn on her arms, face and neck. Now even more disgusted, she limped over to join Marieji under the clump of tall Tua trees by the stable.

Diana settled onto the cool grass and stared blankly at the jungle. *How long have I been here?* she thought. Time seemed to have become a very slippery thing, somehow sliding just out of grasp. Her head pounded from the sun. The dark red blood stain on the riding breeches had spread all the way down to her ankle.

Marieji touched her forearm lightly and held out an orange-yellow fiber canteen. "Drink."

Diana took the canteen and blinked away the sun spots dancing in front of her eyes. She drank long and hard, then bit into a bright yellow fruit Marieji offered. Tiny seeds squished onto her tunic. *Almost like a tomato…*

"Was Corsa hard on you?" Marieji asked.

Diana slumped back against the tree and lifted a hand to gently explore the bump on the back of her head. She was surprised to find it felt smaller – a bit less sensitive. "Hard? I think she wants me to get killed."

"Are you afraid of that horse?"

How could she ask me such a dumb question? Diana looked at Marieji's face and realized that there was laughter behind her eyes. She was being ridiculed. Hot anger flared up. "Get real. Of course I am. I was almost killed by a horse once and–"

"Once? Are you off in the past again?" Marieji wrapped the remaining bread in a soft cloth.

"Hey. What would you do if you'd been–"

"Notice you're speaking about the past again, Diana. Where's your attention?"

Diana sprang angrily to her feet. "I can't stand this stupid game anymore."

"Sit Diana," Marieji patted the grass. "Calm yourself." She hummed a low chant beneath her breath as Diana settled once again down onto the grass.

"Are you still angry?"

"Angry?" she seethed. "Try rage. Hey, it's bad enough to be trapped here, who knows where, in some kind of sick dream. And then you – you ask me if I'm angry? Brother!"

A sudden burst of sound from Marieji exploded in Diana's face. She gasped as anger and fear sliced through her mind like a lightening bolt. A spasm slammed into the base of her spine and snapped vertebrae all the way up into her neck. She collapsed onto her back on the grass, her entire body vibrating.

She was again twelve years old and at Girl Scout camp. A group of girls were riding horseback along a dusty path through a mountain meadow...

Marieji clapped her hands.

The spasms ended as suddenly as they had begun.

Diana sat up and stared open-mouthed at the older woman.

"Wake up Diana. Focus yourself in the present. This is not the same horse, and you are not the same person. Don't allow the past to override the present moment. Take control of your life."

"Yes, but Corsa–"

"This isn't about Corsa. You don't have time to indulge yourself so. Get into the moment and take action. Go finish what Corsa told you to do." Marieji gathered up the carrying bag and canteen, rose and turned toward the main path to the village.

Diana picked the halter up out of the dust, then sucked in her breath when she saw Corsa watching her from the doorway of the stable. "Oh boy," she muttered as the horsewoman started in her direction. "I really, really don't like her."

Corsa slid to a halt directly in front of her. "What happened to your halter?" she snapped, fists on her hips.

Diana gulped at the lump in her throat and shrugged uncomfortably. She attempted to pull up a sense of self confidence, but came up empty handed.

"I guess I dropped it."

Corsa shook her head in obvious disgust. "Looks more like you tried to stomp it to death. What's the matter with you anyway? Get that halter on that mare. Now."

"But I...I can't." Diana protested. She felt her face and neck turn deep red under the pink sunburn.

"Can't?" Corsa spat. "Did I hear you right? Just do it." She grabbed the halter, jammed it into Diana's chest, and strode off toward the stable.

Diana held the halter away from herself at arms' length as though it were a dead snake.

The pox on you, she raged. *I'm a designer, not a cowgirl.*

She stood at the fence and stared at the mare. *I guess I really shouldn't let an old childhood memory control me,* she told herself. *But I'm not into letting that horse stomp me to death, either.*

An old movie scene of a cowboy feeding his horse an apple suddenly slipped into her mind. *That's it,* she thought, *maybe if I offer that horse a piece of fruit or something.*

Diana scanned the corral, then spotted an open sack of oats just inside the stable door. She walked over, slid the halter over her shoulder, filled both of her hands with oats, then slipped back through the corral rails.

"Hey horse." She tried to calm her voice. "I've got something for you."

She set her teeth as the big mare muzzled the oats from her cupped palms, then lifted its head and looked directly at her. A wild thrill burned through her fear. *It worked!*

Diana limped back for more oats, and returned again to

offer them to the mare.

The third time she slid through the corral fence with oats, the big mare whinnied and trotted toward her. Diana braced herself and stood her ground.

"She won't bite you," a male voice called out from behind her.

Diana turned just as Barjo slid through the fence, grinning widely. "Now just loop the rope around her neck, and hold it in place while you slide the halter over her nose."

She held her breath and gently looped the braided rope around the mare's neck. The horse didn't seem to notice.

"OK, now just gently pull the halter up her nose and over her ears," he laughed. "She won't hurt you."

Diana gulped, then cautiously pulled the bottom of the braided halter up over the mare's nose. "Hey," she rasped, "I did it."

"Bribing her with oats will work every time." Barjo reached up and positioned the halter over the horse's ears. "Now lead her around the corral a little bit, then you can walk her around the stable and show Corsa."

* * * * *

"Well, hello." Corsa crossed her arms at the sight of Diana leading the big mare around the corner of the stable. "And what have we here. A baby warrior with her mount? Go ahead and take her back to the corral. Tomorrow we'll see how high she can throw you."

Diana gasped aloud.

Corsa laughed. "Afraid of horses are you? Well then this one really has some big surprises for you."

* * * * *

Diana had decided to avoid the community fire. She sat on the porch of the hut watching the evening light soften the edges of the jungle.

Think, she told herself. *How long have I been here? I'm certain my Earth time must be running out.*

Her thoughts were interrupted when she forgot about the raging sunburn and slapped a mosquito that had landed on her arm.

I've got to get body and mind together, she shuddered. *How can I ride that horse, when I'm scared out of my mind?* The image of a horse running wild across a meadow, pursued by an angry line of bees, played around the edges of her mind.

Diana noted the growing darkness.

"I've got to toughen up," she sighed. She resisted the impulse to flee from the dark into the safety of the hut – instead steeled herself and walked cautiously through the darkness toward the edge of the jungle.

I can do it, she told herself. *Maybe if I just think positively. That's got to be the secret.*

Something large dropped out of a tree just behind her, but she forced herself to stand her ground. She fought off the impulse to just run into the hut.

Finally satisfied she'd made some progress, Diana returned to the safety of the hut, sat on the bed, and listened to the night sounds. A fine whisper of soft fur touched her arm, was gone, then returned with a gentle but insistent push against her hand – Chat Chew.

She reached out and ran her fingers across the finely groomed fur, smiling as the cat arched its back to meet the caress.

Diana settled back onto the pillow.

The cat followed her movement expertly, then pushed a cold nose against her cheek and began to purr in feline rapture.

Diana relaxed even deeper as the cat expanded the volume of her purring, transporting them both into deep sleep.

CR&O

CHAPTER ELEVEN

*Human minds are integrated into the planetary mental system
– the mind of Gaia – which in turn must participate
in some universal or cosmic mind.*

— *Fritjof Capra, PhD*

DIANA PRESSED HER fingers into the tight muscles in the
back of her neck, found they had relaxed some from the day
before. She felt for the lump. *Still tender, but almost gone.*

She felt new confidence from her success the night before,
when she had managed to stand at the edge of the jungle in
total darkness. *Probably nothing to these people,* she thought,
but it feels like a real step forward to me.

She sat down on the porch of the hut to watch the
morning. *Had Earth ever been this beautiful? This pristine?
Could it ever be again?* She sighed a deep, long sigh. *Probably
not in my lifetime.*

After using the outdoor facility shared by the three visitor huts, Diana set out along the path that led to the stable. *I've got to think positive,* she told herself. *I can ride that horse. I can ride that horse. I can...*

Corsa met her at the door of the stable, hands on hips. "Took your time, huh? Get into your boots and pants, then come find me. And snap it up." She shook her head and disappeared into the dark stable.

Diana struggled into the dusty riding pants and boots, then headed for the corral filled with what she hoped was determination. Her mind whirled around one intense thought. *I can ride that horse, I can ride that horse, I can ride...*

She found Barjo and Corsa standing next to the corral gate talking. Corsa looked up, obviously annoyed, looked over at Barjo. "Please make sure this so-called warrior gets onto TwoSox. I'll be back." She turned and walked right past Diana as though she were invisible.

Barjo motioned for Diana to follow him into the tack room. "Are you ready to ride her?" He lifted a halter and lead rope off a wooden peg and handed them to her.

"I don't know," she sighed. "I haven't been on a horse since the time I got my leg broken. I was only twelve and–"

"I don't encourage you to focus on past failures," he interrupted.

"Hey, I'm willing to give it a try."

"A try? OK," he nodded. "Your attitude is at least better. Go put the halter on her."

Her heart pounded wild and hard against her ribs as she slid between the fence rails. *I can do it. I can ride that horse...*

She gulped, then walked directly toward the big mare with the halter in one hand, a handful of oats in the other. Diana was surprised when the bay simply stood calmly and allowed her to slip the halter on its head.

She watched silently as Barjo positioned a well-worn saddle blanket on TwoSox's back, then threw a saddle in place. The mare snorted as he braced his foot against her side to tighten the cinch.

"Likes to hold her breath," he explained. "She wants to control how tight the cinch is." He playfully slapped the side of the mare's neck. "You bad girl. Now you give this Earthie a nice ride, TwoSox."

Corsa reappeared from the stable and nodded impatiently. "So...mount up, warrior."

I can do it, I can do it, I can... Diana sucked in a deep breath, slid her left foot into the stirrup, then swung her right leg over the mare's haunches. For a moment she sat perched in the saddle, her right foot barely in the stirrup.

In the next instant the big mare dropped her head, jerked the reins from Diana's hand, and began to gather herself for action.

Diana grabbed the saddle horn with both hands and jammed her feet deeper into the stirrups.

Time slid sideways, then stopped.

The sound of one particular song bird in a nearby tree echoed through her mind. She heard another bird answer, and then became acutely aware of the morning breeze flowing across her face and the back of her neck.

She heard the sound of laugher drift through the soft white fog that had gathered around her. It sounded as though it came from very far away – somehow from out of her childhood?

She felt the first buck forming under her in slow motion – the deep muscular action as the mare gathered power into her chest and hips. Diana hunkered down and desperately gripped the horse with her legs.

TwoSox exploded up into the air like a tightly coiled spring, landed hard on all four legs, then spun away from the corral fence.

Diana desperately clung to the saddle horn.

The mare reared, then gathered herself for another buck. She landed stiff-legged in the middle of the corral, then kicked up her rear legs.

Both of Diana's feet slid out of the stirrups at the same time. She wildly grabbed the horse's mane with one hand and the saddle horn with the other, then her legs flew into the air as TwoSox spun in a tight circle.

In the middle of the next kick, Diana's life-or-death grip on the saddle horn was torn from her. She hurtled through the air, arms and legs flailing. Her teeth jammed against each other as she landed butt first on the hard-packed surface of the corral.

The mare jumped away stiff-legged, reins dragging in the dust.

"Oh yes," Corsa snorted. "We certainly have a great warrior here." She turned away and left Barjo to pick Diana up out of the dust.

In spite of Barjo's encouragement, Diana absolutely refused to consider going anywhere near the horse.

* * * * *

Diana limped onto the path Barjo had said led to Marieji's hut. The air felt heavy and sultry. *Feels almost like rain,* she thought. *Is it going to rain?* she asked herself. But the raging noise inside her head made a logical answer impossible.

It was now clear to her that positive thinking would get her nowhere. But Marieji said she had to ride. *Had to.* That was the only way to get to the dragon's gate. Every hour, every minute, was beginning to feel more and more precious. "It feels like I'm getting nowhere fast," she sighed.

She found Marieji seated on a low wooden stool on the porch of the hut – a honing stone in one hand, a glistening blade the length of her forearm balanced on her knees.

Marieji smiled at Diana's interest in the sword, gestured with her chin to the stool opposite her. "How did you do with TwoSox?" She shaved the bark off a stick to test the sharpness of the edge.

"Barjo saddled her, and I got up onto her back."

"Oh? And how was your ride?"

Diana silently watched Marieji's deft motions as she honed the edge of the blade.

"Did you have a good ride, Diana?"

"Of course not. That horse tried to stomp me to death."

"Ah…so then, you're going to ride her tomorrow."

Diana shook her head at how out of control her situation was. How totally unreasonable these strange people were determined to be. An emotion beyond anger, beyond fear, beyond reason, rose up into her. "Are you crazy," she exploded. "I'm not getting on that horse again."

"Oh?"

"Look, Marieji – I could have been killed. It was just like when I was a kid and–"

"Still focused in the past, are you?"

"Hey, be reasonable. I went there with a totally positive attitude. But that horse still just threw me off like…like a mosquito. So what should I expect will happen tomorrow? I'll tell you what. She'll just throw me again."

"Certainly if that's what you expect, you won't be disappointed."

"Expect? Oh brother. I don't expect, I know!"

"This is about a lot more than just riding a horse." Marieji sliced open an orange melon and handed half to Diana. "When you visualize something, you actually ensure that it will happen. You could even say that you create it, because you begin to look for evidence that it's happening."

"I told you, Marieji. I used the power of positive thinking. But it didn't get me anywhere."

"Positive thinking? So you tried to convince yourself that something you were certain you'd fail at might instead somehow be possible?"

"Yeah. I guess you could say so. But isn't that what you're telling me to do?"

"Not at all, Diana. So-called positive thinking just alerts your deeper self – informs it that you feel in over your head, and are going to try something you expect to fail at."

That was not what she wanted to hear. Diana tuned Marieji out and looked at the back of her hand, then her forearm. Her sunburn had tempered into a golden tan speckled with tiny flakes of peeling skin. She made a fist, then stared in surprise at the sight of the tendons and newly awakened muscle in her forearm and the inside of her wrist.

"Diana? Please pay attention. What I'm talking about goes far beyond positive thinking. You actually create your entire reality with your thoughts. I mean this literally."

She looked at Marieji, shook her head, and accepted another piece of melon. "Marieji, I don't get what you mean by creating reality. Reality just is, you don't create it."

"Diana, your thoughts, feelings and emotions are really electro-magnetic energy impulses – just like the energy impulses connected to both the Earth, and to the tiniest sub-atomic particle. Your thoughts are real, and they literally build both your body and your entire reality."

"*Build* my body?"

"Yes. Thought waves are just as real as radio and TV waves. Although they're invisible to the naked eye, they actually organize what you call matter on an atomic and sub-atomic level. Just like a magnet attracts iron filings and creates something altogether new – an orderly pile of iron filings. Diana, thinking is actually the most basic creative act. You truly create everything you experience with your thoughts."

"Thinking – a creative act?"

"Oh yes. And here's the point you need to remember – what you focus your attention on determines what you will or won't create with your thoughts. We truly physically create ourselves and our lives – our reality – according to what we pay attention to. Attention is like that magnet – it pulls together and focuses the energy, the organizing power, of our thoughts. Do you understand?"

Diana closed her eyes and tried to grasp what the older woman had said. "I'm not entirely sure."

"Listen carefully. This is really very simple. Your memories, thoughts and feelings are all shaped by where you focus your attention. So you literally create your own reality according to what you pay attention to."

Diana leaned forward intently. "OK. I think I get it."

"Take your childhood experience of being thrown from a horse and breaking your leg," Marieji continued. "When you focus on it today, what you're doing is literally recreating that experience in the present moment. And sure enough, what happened with TwoSox? Just exactly what you expected, and therefore created. You must learn to avoid creating the future based on the past."

"But Marieji, aren't we supposed to learn from our past experience."

"Learn, yes. But recreate the past in the present, no. You are a different person today than you were then. So don't attach past judgments to this new self."

They sat in silence.

"So Marieji, what can I do to stop recreating the past, as you put it?"

"You can no longer be an innocent. The path of the innocent isn't bad, it's just powerless. Moving from the path of innocence to that of the warrior requires a great leap of courage. A warrior can't blame anything outside themselves for the conditions of their life. They realize they are the ultimate creative force in their own life. That's the price of choosing true personal power."

"Uff. That doesn't necessarily sound like a lot of fun," Diana shrugged.

Marieji slid the sword into a leather sheath and nodded. "Perhaps not. But consider your act of coming to the dragon's gate. On a deep level you chose this – a very intense, deeply challenging decision to seek personal power and growth – and to thereby manifest yourself at a much, much higher level of consciousness."

Silence.

"Marieji?"

"Yes?"

"I just hope I'll be able to ride TwoSox tomorrow."

"Hope will get you nowhere with TwoSox," Marieji commented. "Nor will it enable you to stand in the face of the dragon."

"So what's the use then," Diana shrugged.

"You need total intent, my dear warrior. Deep, heartfelt, fully committed, passionate intent. Anything less is totally useless."

"But still I just wish that–"

"There is no power at all in wishing, Diana. You need to absolutely *intend!*"

"But let's face it, Marieji. I'm totally terrified of that horse."

The two sat silently.

"OK." Marieji stood up and stretched, and looked up at the leaden sky. "Let's take a day off from the stables. Tomorrow morning come directly here. Something tells me you may have a serious test of your warrior's intent tomorrow."

* * * * *

Again and again that night the nightmare returned with greater intensity and clarity.

Each time the scorching fire of the dragon's breath fell on her body, her ability to sleep was more deeply destroyed. Diana was finally so distressed that even Chat Chew's persistent purrs failed to have their usual calming effect.

CR&Ͻ

CHAPTER TWELVE

Everything in life can provide nourishment
for some aspect of our being...
if we know how to access that nourishment.

—*Mantak Chia*

KATIE WHITE SLOSHED the tea bag around in the cup of steaming water. She glanced at her friend Douglas Chaffey, also a first year resident at New Community Hospital, then pushed aside the brainwave tracings.

"OK Doug," she shrugged. "I agree that consciousness does imply a certain level of awareness of one's own situation and identity. But who says we can't transfer the focus of our consciousness somewhere else, while our body still remains in the original place?"

"How can that possibly be, White? It's simply not logical," he insisted.

"Come on. Doug. Haven't you ever concentrated so totally on something you forgot everything else happening around you – so that it seemed as though the whole world had just dropped away?"

"Maybe," he shrugged. "Like getting lost in a physiology text and totally losing track of time?"

"That's close." White squeezed the tea bag dry and placed it on a folded napkin, then pushed it safely away from the computer-generated brainwave tracings.

"But how can you compare that to what a shaman goes through in an altered state," he asked. "That seems so totally different. It's not at all the same state of being."

"Well, perhaps a coma is just the extreme of such an experience – an out-of-control extreme, I admit. But maybe a comatose person is so focused on some alternate reality that they lose track of their ordinary reality."

"Huh."

"Or perhaps the problem is that, unlike the shaman and mystic, the comatose person just doesn't know how to return their focus to ordinary reality." Suddenly she snapped her fingers. "Hey Doug, maybe that's what that gap in her signals between low alpha and high theta is all about. Maybe that gap represents a very real physical break between her conscious and unconscious minds. Wow! I hadn't thought of that before."

"You're really into this, aren't you?" he laughed. "So show me some more of what you've got there." He poked at the stack of computer paper with one finger.

White pushed away her cup of tea and unfolded three sheets of continuous computer paper. "Take another look at our Jane Doe with the cranial trauma." She pointed to an area circled in red. "She's an example of what I was talking about.

My two long-term coma cases have extremely flat delta brainwave activity, but look at this."

"Huh. I sure wouldn't call that flat."

"Right. She's extremely active in the theta and delta ranges – very similar to the pattern I've seen for shamans and experienced meditators."

He leaned back in his chair. "Frankly White, I can't see how you make any sense at all out of these tracings."

"You have to get a feel for it, Doug. Take a look at this average for the same period of time." She laid a computer graphic on top of the tracings.

"What's that?"

"It's a pictorial representation of her average readings in the four basic brainwave frequency subsets – beta, alpha, theta and delta."

"Looks like a rough mirror image divided down the middle."

"In a way it is. It shows the balance of brain activities over those frequencies on both sides of the brain."

"I had no idea the technology could do that."

"Look what it shows, Doug. Right at this point she was heavy into theta and delta, but with very little alpha or beta – almost as though she's living in an alternate state of being totally unconnected to her conscious mind, the part of her mind primarily reflected in the alpha and beta frequencies."

"Whew," he whistled. "Has the Bear seen this?"

"He's totally indifferent," she shrugged. "Only reason she hasn't been in for exploratory brain surgery is he was called away to Seattle for a family emergency. But he's due back in three days, and has her rescheduled."

"Too bad. This looks interesting. I'd like to see what these recordings would look like if she regained consciousness."

"There's not much chance of that. If that gap of signals between theta and alpha really does indicate a disconnection between her conscious and unconscious minds, how could she get back? She'd have to accomplish some kind of remarkable quantum leap of consciousness. And how likely is that? Truth is Doug, I doubt this one will be coming back at all."

C@820

CHAPTER THIRTEEN

*Feeling is that aspect of consciousness
which empowers one's intentions.*

—*J. Donald Walters (Kriyananda)*

DIANA WOKE THE next morning when the stars were yet
bright and discovered that the warm spot by her back was Chat
Chew, comfortably nestled right next to her.

"You're a great pal," she whispered into the cat's sable
brown ear. She rolled over, pushed the edge of the blanket
around the cat to form a nest, and slid out of bed.

She selected a piece of fruit from the basket, plopped
down on the stool, and peered looked out the door net at the
early morning. *Reminds me of the way Earth used to look when
I was a kid*, she thought. *I bet it's been over fifty years since
California has seen air this clean.*

The village began to awaken as the first long fingers of

sunlight sliced through the tops of the trees. A group of children gathered around the central well, buckets in hand. Their voices were barely audible above the chattering uproar of the monkeys.

A girl that seemed to Diana to be about twelve or thirteen patiently directed several other children in an orderly drawing of breakfast water from the central well. Diana recalled herself at that age and shook her head. The young girl had an uncanny discipline that had been totally alien to her at that age.

She took a deep breath, noted that the air felt different. Although the morning sky was clear, the breeze felt close – hot and sticky.

Maybe a storm is really coming today, she thought. *But out of a totally clear blue sky?*

She went back into the hut, wrapped two dried fruit bars in a soft cloth and slid them into her tunic pocket, then set out for Marieji's hut.

Diana arrived at the hut just as the older woman emerged from the jungle on another path. Marieji signaled for her to follow.

"To the river?"

Marieji answered with silence.

* * * * *

Diana noticed with satisfaction that she had become better able to keep up with the older woman's challenging pace. *I'm definitely getting stronger,* she thought.

119

"Be present," Marieji said without looking back. "Try to totally focus yourself in the present moment."

Fat rivers of sweat were streaming off Diana's face and down her neck by the time Marieji stopped at the edge of the jungle, right at the foot of a barren cliff.

Marieji pointed to a small spring surrounded by flowering vines. "Drink."

Diana dropped to her knees, thankful for the cool water, then stood and looked for a place to rest.

"Come. You can rest at the top."

"The top?"

Marieji stared at her silently. "Come," she commanded.

"Where?"

Marieji pointed to the cliff. "We're going up."

"Oh no. Not me. I'm not climbing that cliff."

"Are you going to let your fear take over again, Diana? I'll show you how. You'll be fine."

How does this woman know everything I'm afraid of, Diana reflected. *And what makes her think I'd even consider climbing up that—*

"Haven't you climbed before?"

"Marieji, are you kidding? There aren't any cliffs in LA. And even if there were, why would I do such a dumb thing?"

"So you think you can't."

"Think? Hah. I know I can't."

"How is it you know that, since you've never tried it before?"

"I can clearly see it's impossible. That's all."

Marieji put her hands on her hips and laughed playfully.

"All right then, do you remember our conversation about how your thoughts create your reality? Are you willing to try the tools I told you about?"

"Do I have a choice?"

"Go stand at the base of that cliff – face inward."

Diana positioned herself at the base of the cliff as Marieji had asked. *Hope this isn't as big a mistake as I suspect.*

"Now let's experiment with another way of being. You said you can 'see' that you can't climb. Let's find out if your body agrees, Diana. First take a few deep breaths. Now close your eyes and just reach out and touch the side of the cliff with your right hand."

Diana placed her open palm against the side of the cliff.

"Explore it with your fingertips. How does it feel to you?" Marieji asked.

How does it feel? She slid her fingers over the surface of the rock. Her first impression was that it was hard and cold. She tapped it with her fingernails. *No, not that hard.* She gently brushed her fingertips over the surface. The surface was grainy, not as hard as she had expected.

"Now move your fingertips over the rock until you find a place they want to hang on to. Just try it. And keep your eyes closed."

Diana explored the surface of the rock, but failed to find anything to grip. "There isn't any place, Marieji."

"OK. Keep your eyes closed, and slide your hand up a few inches. Find something to hook your fingers into."

Diana inched her fingertips onto the next rock up and found a spot that felt cooler – as though a slight breeze was coming from within. She explored it with her fingers and discovered a crack, then a tiny ledge. She hooked her fingertips onto the ledge. They held.

"Good, keep your fingers there. Now do the same thing with your other hand."

Marieji clapped as Diana hooked the fingers of her left hand around a small outcropping of rock. "Now step up just a little bit and find a place for your right foot."

* * * * *

Diana gently settled her weight on her left foot and tested her footing. She checked the position of her left hand, lifted her right foot to search for a new position, then hesitated. *How far have I climbed?* she wondered.

"Diana, just hold your focus. Don't start thinking about what you're doing. Just do it." Marieji insisted.

But the damage had already been done. Diana opened her eyes and saw Marieji hanging from a tiny ledge right next to her. She looked down and gasped. She was at least ten or twelve feet off the ground. She jammed her belly and chest against the side of the cliff.

"Diana, close your eyes."

She gritted her teeth and shoved her face against the side of the cliff. "No way. Oh no."

"All right. Hang on and I'll go down and find some way to help you." Marieji dropped down the face of the cliff with a few sure movements.

Diana felt dizzy and frozen stiff with fear. She heard

Marieji at the base of the cliff, but avoided looking down.

"Diana," Marieji suddenly shouted. "Climb...now...fast."

Diana looked down just as Marieji threw herself at the face of the cliff – a huge panther right behind her. The cat leapt up against the side of the cliff trying to snag Marieji's foot.

There was no safety except up.

Marieji propelled herself up the face of the sheer cliff and threw her body over the top. She rolled over and stretched her hands down to Diana.

Something deep inside of Diana demanded action. With a powerful gasp she threw her body upward against the face of the cliff. Fingers and toes dug into the rock, slipped, found holds. Her breath ran ahead of her – pulled her upward.

She heard the big cat scrambling behind her, and pushed even harder. A strong hand grabbed her right wrist and pulled her the rest of the way to the top.

Diana rolled over onto her belly and looked over the cliff. The panther was gone. *How could it disappear so fast?* She turned to Marieji and was greeted by twinkling eyes.

"Marieji. What?"

"Still think you can't climb?" she smiled.

"But, the panther?"

"Was never there, Diana All I had to do was suggest it, and your fear took over and manifested one. That's what I mean by creating our own reality."

Diana sat back on her haunches and stared at the older woman. The reality of what she had seen was undeniable. Equally undeniable was the fact that the big cat was not there. She searched inside herself for some other answer, found none.

"You made a fool of me, Marieji."

"No, not a fool. I just helped you discover how powerful a passionate intention can be. Solid intention burns right through fear – even uses fear to fuel itself. Am I right? Didn't your intent to survive get you right up the face of the cliff?"

Diana shook her head, speechless.

"Let's just rest for a while, Diana. Then I'll show you why I brought you here."

* * * * *

Diana rested uneasily. When she woke the sun had disappeared entirely behind a thick bank of gray-bottomed clouds; she was sweating from the sultry moisture hanging in the air. She sat up and found Marieji watching her from a few feet away. The light seemed somehow very odd.

"Rested? Come join me, Diana. There's something I want to show you."

She squatted down next to Marieji and looked at the two pieces of bamboo she had pulled from her belt pouch. "What are those for?"

"Here, have a drink." Marieji held out a canteen. "Then I'll show you."

Diana gulped lukewarm water from Marieji's canteen, chewed ravenously on her remaining dried fruit bar.

"Now Diana, you find it hard to believe that everything is made up of the same energy. Is that true?"

"Yes and no," Diana frowned. "I understand that my body is supposedly made up of molecules in motion, and scientists claim the basic nature of reality is really not physical at all." Diana held up her hand. "But truthfully Marieji? This body doesn't look like it's just energy to me. It looks just as solid as can be."

"Want to experiment with what you're seeing, Diana?"

"Huh, I don't know. I don't think I can handle any more of your tricks today, Marieji."

"No panthers, Diana. Something special I want you to experience. Just relax, listen and watch." Marieji began to tap the two pieces of bamboo together in an odd rhythm.

Diane settled her back against a rock and focused on the reverberating sound. The clicking sounds of the bamboo seemed to echo around them. It seemed to her that the insects and the wind were keeping time with the rhythm – as though even her brain wanted to follow the rhythm, like a heartbeat.

Marieji began to make a strange clicking sound along with the bamboo.

Diana blinked, then blinked again. It seemed as though she could see right through Marieji's body. Then she realized that in fact she could. She glanced down at her own hand and gasped. It was surrounded by an envelop of shimmering light. She could see right through the skin, could clearly see the blood flowing in bursts through the blood vessels in her hand.

It all felt very familiar.

The sound entrained her mind into a vaguely familiar vibration and a feeling of deep ecstasy flowed through her

She felt herself become one with nature – with the entire mountain. Then she remembered how as a young child she used to soften her vision, defocus somehow, and see right into things. She remembered seeing right into the pure energy of life, just as she was at this very moment.

* * * * *

Marieji tied her canteen onto her belt, then tapped Diana lightly on the shoulder. "Time to go. The sky is about to open."

Diana rubbed her eyes in disbelief as Marieji leapt off the plateau, bounced lightly off three outcropping rocks, then landed lightly at the base of the twenty-foot cliff.

Marieji pointed to a narrow trail Diana had failed to see on the way up. "If you're afraid to follow me, come down that way," she laughed.

Diana trembled from her fearful half-hour descent down the narrow path. "How did you do that?"

"Do what?" Marieji shrugged.

"Get down that cliff like that?"

"I used my warrior's intent and just did it."

"Intent? But it looked like you were flying."

"No. Just passionate intent."

Intent? More like magic. She's playing word games with me again, Diana scowled.

Marieji laughed her deep laughter. "Not magic or games, Diana. Just warrior's intent. Like what got you up the face of that cliff today."

"You mean having your life threatened?"

"No. It's more like fueling your desire with passionately felt emotion. That's what turns a desire into an intention. And if you apply enough deeply felt emotion to an intention, you truly become your intent. Then nothing can stand in your way or prevent you from achieving your goal."

"I'm afraid that's over my head," Diana protested. "I never went in for that psychology stuff. I just wish I had–"

"No more wishes," Marieji boomed. She bent over, grabbed a huge rock and lifted it above her head.

Diana gasped at the older woman's raw strength.

"There is no power in wishes. Do you *wish* that I not crush your skull with this rock?" Marieji roared.

Diana threw herself sideways. The rock flew past where she had stood just a moment before and smashed against another rock with such force that Diana felt the ground tremble.

"Intent," Marieji roared again. You must feel it so completely that you become your intent. Feed your desire with deeply felt emotion – then you create the power of intention."

Diana stared into Marieji's dark eyes. They flashed with a strange, deeply powerful light.

"Your intent must burn within you. And you must use it to totally replace your fear with power. Mere wishes are a worthless waste of the life force. Only intent has power and value."

Diana stood speechless, deeply shocked. She only vaguely noticed the huge drops of steaming rain that had begun to pockmark the dust around them.

"Can you find your way back to the village by yourself?"

"No," Diana shook her head. "No, I'm certain I can't."

"Good. Then you'll have to use your warrior's intent. I'm

going far out in front of you, Diana. You will have to reach out for the village with passionate intent. Unless, of course, you'd rather spend the next few days and nights out here alone in the jungle."

"Oh please, Marieji. I can't do—"

"Just let go of your fear and intend to follow me. It's all energy, Diana." She reached out and patted Diana's solar plexus. "Just reach out for the village from here."

Diana saw a bright flash of luminescent light shoot out of Marieji's solar plexus, then watched her soar fifty feet down the path without moving her feet.

"Reach out with your intent." Marieji shouted, then disappeared from sight.

Diana lurched onto the path and ran toward where she had seen Marieji. She stopped where two paths intersected. The rain drops had raised tiny craters in the dusty path. There was no trace of Marieji's footprints.

Cold streams of sweat ran down the inside of Diana's arms. "No footprints," she stammered. "This is impossible. How could she move so fast?"

A booming clap of thunder slapped against the sky, loosening a blinding sheet of rain.

Diana panicked, then felt a tugging sensation in her solar plexus – as though some invisible force was pulling her toward the path to the right.

She resisted the unfamiliar sensation with her logical mind. "Not sure that's the right way." The tugging sensation instantly fell away.

"Intent," she gasped. "I intend to follow Marieji." The

tug in her solar plexus returned, this time even stronger. She bounded onto the path, following the odd feeling in her gut at each turn.

* * * * *

When she finally reached the river her clothing was plastered to her skin with a mixture of the warm rain and wide rivulets of salty sweat. Diana followed the tugging sensation upstream, dropping to her knees in exhaustion when she recognized the villagers' bathing beach on the other side of the river.

Diana struggled against the rising waters and crossed to the safety of the village, then went immediately to her hut. Chat Chew was stretched out in full feline comfort on the bed.

Dry clothes, a small loaf of bread, and a covered container of stew were on the table. A note from Marieji was on the stack of clothing. "You must use your intent to ride TwoSox tomorrow. Your time is contracting rapidly," it read.

CHAPTER FOURTEEN

*A telescopic view of one thousand light years into
space appears almost identical to a microscopic view
of a human cell enlarged to one angstrom.*

—*Philip & Phyllis Morrison*

*BE IN THE moment, become your intent. Be in the moment,
become your intent. Be in the moment…* Diana woke with the
phrase she had gone to sleep on still repeating in her mind.

She sat up and seized Chat Chew's flickering tail.
"Remember to be in the moment and become your intent, Chat
Chew." She gave the cat's tail a tug. "Look what it got me
through."

Diana arrived at the stable just as the Morning Parrot
shrieked its third wake up call. She filled the pockets of her
shorts with oats and headed straight for TwoSox's corral.

The mare trotted over to her. But when Diana failed to

immediately offer a second handful, TwoSox switched her tail, shook her head, and high stepped to the far side of the corral.

"You really are one beautiful creature," Diana sighed. "I just hope that–" She caught herself mid sentence. "Intent. Intent. Intent. I intend to ride you today, TwoSox."

By the time Barjo arrived, Diana had changed into her boots and riding breeches and was balanced on the top rail of the fence. She followed along behind him into the stable to tend to a newly born foal.

* * * * *

It was mid-morning before they headed to the tack room for a saddle and bridle. Barjo lifted a halter and lead rope off a peg and handed them to Diana. "Well," he asked. "Are you ready to ride TwoSox?"

"I intend to do so."

"My, my." Barjo laughed. "The warrior appears."

"I do," Diana stressed as they walked toward the corral.

"Oh, I believe you," he smiled, "but you also have to take TwoSox's intentions into consideration. No one has ridden her in almost a year."

"I intend to ride her."

"OK. Corsa should be here any minute. Marieji told her you were to ride today, no matter what."

"Fine." Diana slid between the rails and strode, heart pounding, directly toward the mare. TwoSox looked up, switched her tail, and watched her approach.

Diana pulled a handful of oats from her pocket and held out her cupped palm. To her relief, she managed to slip the halter over the mare's head without incident. She was again relieved when TwoSox allowed her to lead her over to the fence where Corsa and Barjo stood talking.

Corsa nodded indifferently at Diana, then turned to Barjo. "Saddle her up."

* * * * *

Barjo looked Diana full in the eyes, then silently handed her the reins.

She breathed a long, deep sigh to release her gnawing tension, then reminded herself of successfully scaling the cliff and finding her way back to the village alone. *Just be in the moment and become your intent*, she told herself. *I intend to ride this horse.*

Corsa kicked impatiently at the dust. "So, mount up," she snapped. "I don't have all day to just stand around and wait for you to get on that horse."

Diana took a deep breath, wrapped the reins securely around her left hand, slid her left foot into the stirrup, and quickly swung her right leg over the mare's haunches. She jammed her right foot securely into the stirrup, grabbed the saddle horn, and waited for the horse to explode.

The mare whinnied, pulled a couple of times against the bit, then shook her head in surprise to find a tight hand on the reins.

Diana held her breath when the mare snorted and pawed at

the dust, then shook her head even harder. She tightened her grip on the saddle horn, braced herself, and waited. "I intend to ride you, TwoSox," Diana rasped.

The mare cocked her ears at the sound of Diana's voice, stamped at the dust and snorted explosively, then stood quietly.

"Well, fry me a lizard liver." Corsa exclaimed. "What's this?"

Diana cautiously leaned over and patted TwoSox on the neck. "Hey TwoSox," she whispered. "I'm sorry I was such a jerk the other day."

"Ride her around the corral, Diana," Barjo said quietly. "Just pull the reins gently over her neck in the direction you want her to go. Be firm. You don't want to confuse her."

"Stay with her Barjo," Corsa spat. "She's likely to be eating dust any minute." She turned and left.

Diana followed Barjo's suggestion and gently pulled the reins to her right. The mare shook her head in protest, then moved out in the indicated direction.

"Barjo. I just can't believe it," Diana exclaimed. "How am I doing this?"

"Looks like your intent is stronger than your fear, Diana. Great job. You gave TwoSox a very different message than the other day."

She beamed at him from atop the mare.

* * * * *

The sun was in the mid-day sky when Sola, Marieji's apprentice, appeared at the corral and called to her. Barjo took the mare, and Diana changed and joined the younger woman on the grass.

"I've brought food," Sola smiled. "And this is for you... from Marieji." She handed Diana a net bag containing a belt, a hand-forged knife with an intricately carved bone handle and a leather sheath, and a large bar of yellow soap.

Diana ran the belt through the loops on her shorts, positioned the sheathed knife on her right side. She pulled the bar of soap out of the bag. "Guess this is a comment."

"Oh, that's not for you," Sola blushed. "Marieji asked me to show you where to wash your clothes. That's washing soap. Let's eat, then we can get your dirty clothes and I'll take you down river so you can wash them."

* * * * *

Diana retrieved her dust-caked riding pants and walked with the younger woman back to the hut. She dragged her bag of dirty clothes out from beneath the table – leapt backward when the red-bellied lizard, now without a tail, fell out of her dirty clothes and scrambled for cover.

The path they followed was unfamiliar. Diana thought that they had turned away from the river, and was surprised to discover that they had climbed above a small waterfall. Just beyond the waterfall she followed Sola through a tunnel cut through an especially dense section of the lush jungle vegetation.

This must be what it's like in the Amazon, Diana thought.

So beautiful and wild. She followed Sola out of the tunnel into a sunny clearing next to a calm section of the river. A large bamboo structure stood out at the far end of the rocky beach.

"Marieji told me to tell you that once you've washed and dried your clothes, the rest of the afternoon is yours. But be sure to come back to the village with the others. She'll skin me if you get lost or hurt out here in the jungle."

"It's OK, Sola. I'm very much aware that this place is full of nasty little surprises."

"Just remember to be fully conscious when you're out of the village." She lifted a wooden bucket and ridged board from the collection of wash boards stacked in the bamboo shed. "Want me to show you how to use them?"

"I'm sure I can figure it out," Diana shrugged.

A group of three young women giggled among themselves as they watched Diana struggle with the washboard. Finally one of them got up and walked across the beach toward her.

"Mind if I help?" The young woman squatted down next to Diana, gently coaxed the washboard from her hands. "Like this." She soaked a pair of shorts in the bucket, slapped them onto the ribbed washboard, then rubbed the bar of soap over them several times.

"Oh boy. Guess I've got a lot to learn."

"Just up and down a few times." The young woman rubbed the shorts vigorously against the board, dipped them into back into the bucket, and repeated the process. Then she handed the washboard to Diana and stood up to pick a large leaf from a nearby tree. She put the shorts on the leaf and placed it on the sand next to Diana. "Just rinse them in the river when you're done," she smiled.

Diana finished washing her clothes and rinsed them in the river, then followed the example of the other women and arranged them on the large rocks to dry in the sun. One of the young women walked past her to a berry bush at the end of the beach. Diana watched out of the corner of her eye as the woman picked a handful of red berries.

Her mouth watered. *Berries. Yes.*

She ambled over as casually as she could and picked a single berry off the prickly bush. The juice stained her finger red, but the sweet burst in her mouth prodded her on. She picked a large leaf and washed it in the river, loaded it with the berries, then settled down onto the warm sand to wait for her clothes to dry.

The peaceful sounds of the river and the younger women's laughter lulled her into a comfortable nap.

* * * * *

Diana woke and found herself alone at the river – the sun low behind the trees. Anxiety fluttered all over her body. She clearly remembered how it had felt to be alone in the badlands.

A line of sweat instantly formed on her upper lip. She leapt up, snatched her clothes off the rocks, stuffed them into the net bag, then glanced at the sun.

Maybe half an hour of daylight left, she estimated. *It took us longer than that to get here. And I'll never find my way back in the dark,* she shuddered. *Never!*

She slung the bag over her shoulder and hurried toward the path winding back into the dense jungle.

Diana stumbled to a stop where a huge limb had fallen over the path. It had grown more and more difficult to see in the dark green twilight. *Was that limb there before*, she asked herself. *Is this the right path?* Another path led to the left. Nothing seemed familiar.

"Great! Just great," she muttered. She was dizzy, hot, confused. *Just get moving*, she told herself. *Get moving and think.* She jumped at the snap of a twig just a few feet away, then made an instant choice of the unblocked path.

The path ended abruptly at the edge of a small pool barely visible through a mass of tangled vines hanging down from the surrounding trees. *Think*, she demanded. *Don't panic, just think. Maybe I should start a fire,* she thought. *No matches! I've got to get back to the village. Intent*, her inner self reminded her. *Use your intent.*

Something moved on a vine on the other side of the small pool. A snake as thick as Diana's wrist dropped off into the dark water. "That does it," she gasped. "I've got to get out of here, now!"

She backed away from the pool a couple of steps, then hesitated to listen for any evidence of the village. But there were no human voices to be heard. Every sound of the jungle had become a lurking danger.

The snake slithered out of the water and onto the bank about ten feet from where she stood.

"Cripes," she gasped. She spun around, leapt back onto the path, and ran back to where the large limb had fallen over the trail.

"This has to be the right way," she reassured herself. She pushed her way through the tangled branches to the other side of the limb.

The net bag snagged on one branch after another as she tried to race along the trail. A steady river of cold sweat dripped down her neck and inner arms. She stumbled over a root that had grown across the path, landed hard on her hands and knees, and immediately jumped to her feet to listen for any signs of human voices.

Instead she heard the crunch of leaves just a few feet behind her. The jungle was already too dark to make out the source of the sound. She dropped her bag of clothes and dove behind a large tree next to the trail.

She immediately regretted leaving her bag in full view. Something was sniffing the air for her scent. She could feel it scanning the jungle, planning its attack. She peered around the tree. Nothing was visible in the increasingly dark jungle. Her leg muscles trembled. *I can't just stay here. I've got to make a run for it.*

She sucked in a ragged breath and peered around the tree again. Still nothing. A wild desperation raged inside her. *I've got to get out of here. Now!*

She jumped out from behind the tree and grabbed her bag of clothes, then froze and listened.

She could feel eyes pinning her.

Another twig snapped.

Diana held her breath, but overcame the impulse to run. *Use your intent,* her mind screamed at her. *Just calm down and use your intent.*

Even the faintest sound had become magnified.

Suddenly aware of a slight tugging sensation in her solar plexus, she lifted one foot and stepped forward as quietly as possible. The tugging sensation increased. She began to walk as fast as possible without losing the path in the growing darkness.

She felt she had gone further than the village should have been when again something rustled in the thick underbrush. Diana froze, then recognized the faint sound of human voices. She sniffed the air, and recognized a trace of cooking fires. The village?

"Diana?"

Diana jumped wildly at the sound of Sola's voice calling out to her, then again heard another twig snap. She froze and lifted a finger to her lips to signal for silence.

Sola stood motionless and scanned the underbrush for the source of danger. Finally satisfied, she quietly moved to join Diana on the path, then motioned for Diana to follow her to the village clearing one cautious step at a time.

"I see you're practicing moving in full awareness," the younger woman commented as they stepped into the clearing.

"Moving in full awareness?" Diana exploded. "Something was following me."

Sola defocused her eyes and extended her senses back out

into the jungle. She pointed to a pair of slanted eyes peering out at them from the thick underbrush at the edge of the jungle. "Is that the something?"

Realizing she'd been spotted, Chat Chew leapt from her hiding place and raced into the clearing, playfully jumped sideways to challenge the two women, then raced back into the jungle.

"I'll kill her," Diana gasped. "She scared me almost to death back there."

"So you got a taste of how fear can twist reality? Chat Chew is truly a skilled stalker. Maybe you should take some lessons from her," Sola laughed.

Just as Diana stepped onto the porch of the hut, Chat Chew again raced out of the jungle and jumped at her sideways to announce her challenge.

"OK," Diana shouted at the cat. She hurled her bag of clothes through the door of the hut. "This time you're dead meat."

She raced after the cat, chasing her along the path toward the river until the Siamese suddenly disappeared in the darkness.

CHAPTER FIFTEEN

*Do you wish to wake at the moment of your death
and realize you haven't even fully tasted life?
Be here now.*

—*Alan Watts*

FOR THE TENTH time that morning Marieji sprang from the
jungle behind her and pushed Diana off her feet and down onto
the sand.

She sat up and spat out a thick mixture of sand and blood.
"That's it." A wild light flashed from Diana's eyes. "This is
just plain stupid."

"Quitting?"

"You got it." Diana drew herself to her feet, kicked at
the wooden sword, and stalked to the edge of the river to wash
out her mouth.

"Diana?"

Diana spat blood onto the sand. "Look. I'll never learn
your so-called warrior's stance." *What use could this have*

anyway? She's playing games with me again, Diana seethed.

"Feeling skeptical?" Marieji motioned for Diana to join her in the shade.

"Hah. You noticed. How very, very intuitive of you, Marieji."

"Diana, life just passes right by skeptics."

She stood silently and clenched her teeth. *Geez,* Diana protested to herself *Here comes another lecture. Why can't she just leave me alone?*

Marieji laughed one of her long, deep laughs. "Skepticism is just another name for fear, Diana."

"Here it comes," she sighed.

"The skeptic remembers having been hurt some time in the past. They are afraid of being hurt again. So they close down their ability to be spontaneous and flow with life. Is that how you want to be?"

"Hey, think it's fun to eat sand? I have a right to be skeptical." *Hurt?* she seethed to herself. *How about having an old woman make a total fool of you?*

"Better to let go and step into the face of your fear. Then your mistakes and failures become opportunities to grow, instead of something to be feared."

"Sure," Diana snapped. "So I should just stand there and hope you won't push my face in the sand again?"

"You could try trusting yourself."

"Oh great, Marieji. That sounds like great fun. Very, very productive. And you wonder why I'm feeling skeptical?"

"Yes. I do. It indicates to me that on a very deep level you really don't trust yourself."

"Hah." Diana spat more blood into the sand. "It's a lot more than that. Why not just jump off a cliff or walk into a burning building. I'd have more chances of success than I do with this."

Marieji's powerful laughter echoed around her. "Does your ability to stand present with a wooden sword in hand seem so impossible to you?"

"You want to know the truth?" Diana snapped. "It's just like when I was a kid. My best friend made fun of me when I tried to play field hockey. I never could learn to hit the ball right. I was always afraid that the other players would just put me down like she did, so I–"

Marieji held up her hand. "Do you hear what you're saying Diana?"

"Now what?"

"Your skepticism has little to do with the challenge of standing in full consciousness with a wooden sword. It instead has to do with recreating an old fear."

"Oh no, not again." Diana could almost hear her girlhood friend's scornful words. Could clearly recall the look of disgust on her face when she had struggled to handle the hockey stick. *The stupid stick just was too long for me.*

Marieji looked directly at her. "Diana, I don't see any hockey sticks around here. Do you? So why are you carrying an old fear around as if had some value?"

"Huh. As if I had a choice." *Why won't she just stay out of my face? Stop pushing at me like this? Gads, she reminds me of my Third Grade teacher.*

"You feel you don't have a choice? Whose life is this

anyway?" Marieji looked around for evidence that someone else was with them.

"Come on, Marieji. Can't you just let off for once?"

"How many times must we deal with this issue, Diana? Does someone else control your choices?"

"Marieji," Diana seethed, "this isn't a joke."

"I'm not joking. All of this is just an attempt to avoid being hurt – or to avoid feeling put down, as you put it. So you create skepticism to protect yourself from being hurt again, Diana. And so it goes…on and on."

Diana set her teeth and wrapped her arms around herself. She was getting nowhere. No matter what she tried, it always seemed to end up like this. *Perhaps I should just give up,* she thought.

Marieji shook her head sadly. "The shadow of the past is darkening the light of the present. You need to let go – hold your focus in the present moment."

"The shadow of the past? Hah, Marieji. Now you're really making me mad."

"Diana," Marieji put her hand on Diana's arm. "Have I opened such a sensitive wound? All this over being pushed down into the sand? I think not. What you really fear is that your pride will be damaged, just like it was so many years ago."

"Hey. It's no fun to eat sand."

Marieji picked up the wooden sword and held it out to Diana. "Stop recreating the past. Just let it go. Be here now – in the present moment."

"OK," Diana shrugged, "you don't have to rub it in."

"Are you ready to try again?"

"Crap." Diana grabbed the wooden sword from Marieji's hand. "Show me again how to stand in that warrior's stance. Maybe I can forget you just shoved my face into the sand for the umpteenth time this morning."

Diana positioned her feet at shoulder's width and flexed her knees, then let Marieji adjust the angle of her feet slightly.

"Flex your knees a bit more," Marieji suggested. "Good. Now just balance lightly on your feet. Don't stop to think, just let your body respond to what it senses. Now close your eyes, and be present."

Diana closed her eyes and felt the pungent, warm breeze gently lift the ends of her hair. She noted the shadow of a bird flying overhead as the sunlight falling on her closed eyelids was momentarily interrupted. Above the fluctuating sounds of the flowing water she picked out the distinctive whoosh of a dragonfly...the buzz of a fly...then the plaintive cry of a hawk.

She sighed to release her tension and relax the muscles of her stomach. Recalling Marieji's instructions, she pulled a deep breath down into the bottom of her lungs and exhaled slowly through her nose. Then she flexed her knees even deeper and curled her toes down into the sand.

Her eyes flew open the moment the first dry leaf crunched. She spun around to face the threat, but no one was there.

Diana defocused her eyes and extended her senses out into the jungle to identify the source of the crunching leaves. She listened deeply, her eyes combing the trees and underbrush, but found nothing but undulating patterns of light and shadow.

Suddenly she noticed a subtle interruption in the flow of the cooler breeze coming off the river. She dropped her weight and spun around. There stood Marieji – hands raised, and about to push her face down into the sand.

"Hah," she jabbed the wooden sword into the older woman's gut.

Marieji laughed, then fell backward and slapped the sand with both hands.

Diana yelped with joy, threw the wooden sword in the air and dove down onto the sand next to her.

* * * * *

Marieji called for a swim in the river.

"You know, Marieji," Diana sighed as they lay in the warm sand to dry. "I'm still not sure I totally understand how I ended up here on Gaia."

"Look at the river, Diana. See how the water meets obstacles, and simply flows over or around them? Life is just like the river – a flowing dance of constantly changing pure energy."

Silence.

Diana broke the silence. "But how can I physically be here on Gaia? Do you mean that my energy somehow changed?"

"That's one way to understand it. But what initiated the change was where you choose to focus your consciousness."

Diana slapped an open palm against her own leg.

"But how," she asked, "did this body end up here?"

"Remember that your body is an organized center of

constant creation and destruction from the very moment you're conceived."

"That's an interesting theory."

"Not theory, fact." Marieji reached over and gently pinched a fold of skin on the back of Diana's hand. "In less than a month, every one of these skin cells will have died and been replaced by new cells. And by the end of this year, almost every cell in your body will be new."

"OK, but that still doesn't explain how I ended up here on Gaia."

"Ah. The secret is in the very structure of life itself. As you now know, what we call matter is actually energy in constant transformation. There's really very little truly solid stuff at all."

"Are you trying to tell me this rock isn't solid," Diana asked, slapping her hand against a rock.

"Yes."

"Then why doesn't my hand just pass right through it?"

"One of the characteristics of atoms, which are really just little organized energy systems," Marieji continued, "is that their components move rhythmically. They set up vibrational waves – just like the string of a guitar when you pluck it. Do you follow me?"

"I think so."

"So although the rock is made up of a few atoms with a lot of space in between them, the rock's atoms set a stable pattern of vibrational waves that resists being interrupted. You might say its similar to a force field."

"So…that vibration is something like an invisible barrier?"

"Right. And the same is true of your body. Your cells are also made up of atoms and sub-atomic particles – everything is just energy in motion. Do you understand?"

Diana nodded thoughtfully.

"But your body doesn't have a well organized crystalline force field like the rock. It's rather a collection of interrelated energy fields that constantly change in response to each other and the environment."

"But what holds it all together?"

"The same life force holds both you and the rock together. There is only one form of life energy."

"How can that be?"

"Diana, life is basically a dance of relationships between interacting, vibrating energy systems that are all connected to the same source – like a web."

"But Marieji, that still doesn't explain how I ended up here on Gaia."

"You ended up here because you changed the level of your basic vibration. Instead of vibrating at Earth's vibratory level, you somehow focused part of your being into Gaia's vibratory level. Just like jumping from one musical octave to another – you made a vibratory quantum leap."

Diana sat upright and looked at Marieji intensely. "But how in blazes did I do that?"

"Look at it this way – your personal being is governed by the same rules as the rest of the life. As you know, atoms are surrounded by frequency bands where sub-atomic bundles of energy reside, just like the frequency bands that hold the planets in position around the sun."

Diana shifted so she could look directly into Marieji's eyes. "Like what holds the moon in rotation around Earth?"

"That's right. Each atom, each planet, and the core of each universe, is encircled by bands of energy – and these bands all vibrate at different, but interrelated levels. Just like the vibrational notes of a musical scale. Your being follows the same rule, and is also surrounded by several vibrating energy bands. Many traditional mystics have referred to these bands as the different 'dimensions' of reality."

Diana settled back down onto the sand. "So it seems as though the mystics and scientists are really saying the same thing."

"They are. But one major difference between you and that rock," Marieji continued, "is that you can make a conscious choice to focus your being at any of your potential vibratory levels, or dimensions. But the rock doesn't have the conscious ability to initiate such a change. It is largely governed by the action of outside forces and events. You, on the other hand, can choose to change…or not to change."

"And?" Diana encouraged her to continue.

"That's how people of Earth accomplish both powerful creative acts, and feats of great genius and bravery," Marieji replied quietly. "They make quantum leaps in their vibratory levels."

Diana stared silently and shook her head. "What do you mean – quantum leaps?"

"They focus on a higher vibratory level or dimension – tap into a broader aspect of the unified energy system we call life. There is nothing mysterious about this, Diana. A change of focus is also at the core of what you refer to as out-of-the-body experiences, astral travel, deep meditation, mystical insights, and even the transition you call death."

"So is that how I got here on Gaia? I made a quantum leap?"

"In essence. But in your case it wasn't the result of a conscious decision or intention. Your leapt because you were totally overwhelmed by great personal stress."

Boy is that true, Diana admitted to herself. *I was totally stressed out.*

"For this same reason, many in your times choose to lose themselves in violent acts, or turn to mind-altering drugs and alcohol, and even insanity. It's not that they're bad people. They are simply overwhelmed just like you were, and simply unable to change or adapt."

"But my fall?"

"Your fall wasn't really the cause, Diana. You collapsed because you were already out of focus. The parade and the dragon were only what you would call 'the final straw.' To survive, your higher self leapt to the next comfortable energy level. Focusing your consciousness here on Gaia was an unconscious survival choice."

"But why can't I just go back? Why all this about facing a dragon and going through some gate. Can't I just choose to refocus myself back on Earth?"

Marieji leaned back and took a deep breath. "Diana, falling unconsciously from one level to another is one thing; but consciously altering the vibratory level of your being is quite another. It requires the ability to fully focus your conscious in the moment, and the strength to face a great moment of truth in which you may face almost certain death."

"So…no matter what, I'm going to die?"

"You may or may not. But when you step up to face the dragon, you'll face the naked truth of your being. Whether or not you can survive that, I can't say. Many fail, while a few succeed."

"Whoa!"

"In the final moment you'll come face to face with everything you've ever sought to avoid – who you really are behind all the fear, anxiety and regret that claims to own you."

"I really don't like the sound of that," Diana muttered. "I really don't."

"That's why so few choose the warrior's path. Every being knows the truth of this on a soul level. Most choose to remain on the path of the innocent, rather than step onto the warrior's path and seek the truth of their being."

An odd *deja vu* slipped through Diana's mind. "Somehow that sounds familiar. As though I've heard that before."

"You certainly heard it when the dragon called to you, and you chose on a higher level to answer. Many hear that call and choose not to respond. You should thank yourself for creating such an awesome growth opportunity, Diana. How would you instead like to wake at the moment of your death and realize you hadn't even really been fully alive?"

Diana ran her fingers through her hair. "But you said I may not live through this."

"True. The time you have to prepare is fading rapidly.

We need to move you along more rapidly than I wish."
Tomorrow we'll trade that wooden sword in for a warrior's
blade. For certain you aren't totally ready, Diana. But if you
can't survive the swordmaster, you wouldn't survive the
dragon anyway."

"Survive the swordmaster?" Diana choked.

"Yes. You no longer have the luxury of letting your
consciousness wander," Marieji said slowly. "You had best
learn to be fully present in the moment, fast."

"Or?"

"Yorrow, the swordmaster, may very well simply cut
you down."

☙❧

CHAPTER SIXTEEN

*At first, when you make the choice to
let go of your old patterns, it may appear that
things in your life are falling apart.*

—*Shakti Gawain*

DR. KATIE WHITE and a nurse stood silently at the end of the bed looking at Diana's still body. White broke the silence. "Why haven't you removed those wrist restraints?"

"Can't," the nurse replied, "the admitting ER doc ordered them, and it's still on her chart."

"Let's see." White coaxed the chart from the nurse's hand. "OK. Here it is. Still, it does seem ridiculous. Is she still thrashing?"

"No. Not at all. She's starting to look like the long-term comas up in Ward C."

"Oh well," White sighed, "the life of a Jane Doe."

She handed back the chart and slid her portable computer onto the metal tray next to the bed, jacked into the feedback monitor, and deftly keyed in instructions for a brainwave printout.

* * * * *

Interns White and Chaffey bent over the brainwave tracings.

"Look at this, Doug," White circled a portion of the tracings with a red marker. "Her brainwaves are focused almost entirely in upper delta and lower theta now – primarily around four to five cycles-per-second."

"Looks like a coma to me."

"No. It's different." She dropped two other tracings on the table and opened them. "See. She's in a much narrower frequency band, and there are hardly any variations. I ran a statistical analysis on her readings. The variation is much less on the right side of her brain than on the left."

"So," he pulled up a chair.

"Doug, this reminds me of something I remember reading in Robert Monroe's *Journeys Out of the Body*."

"You mean that guy who claimed he could leave his body and travel consciously to other places?"

"Right."

"Why do you say that. What's the..."

"I remember that a psychiatrist ran brainwave studies on Monroe during some of his out-of-the-body experiences."

"And?"

"He reported the same pattern. A tight focus of brainwave frequencies in the four to five cycles-per-second range, and no spikes at all above ten. I think he also reported a statistically significant difference between the right and left hemispheres."

"Are you saying that you think she's–"

"Experiencing an extended out-of-the-body experience? Yes, that's what I'm saying."

"Oh no. What if you're right and–"

"Right, Doug. She's scheduled for a low-survivability surgical procedure."

"Gads, White. Have you shown this to the Bear?"

"Tried to. He just shrugs it off. She's scheduled for surgery in two days."

CHAPTER SEVENTEEN

In Chinese, the word "crisis" is composed
of two characters – one represents danger,
and the other represents opportunity.

—*John F. Kennedy*

THERE WAS NO possible escape.

The swordmaster was poised for the kill – the tip of his blade less than a hand's width from her stomach.

After two solid weeks of aggressive sparring with naked blades, Diana had made the fatal mistake.

She was going to go down unless–

Her mind went blank; totally void of thought.

An unearthly sound sheared through her mind. Diana froze, then felt herself fly apart as the space between her cells exploded outward at the speed of light.

She looked down and realized her body had become totally transparent. She heard breathing, then realized it was her own breath, magnified a thousand-fold.

Before her stood Yorrow, frozen in mid thrust like a life-sized figure in a wax museum – the tip of his blade poised only inches from her unprotected stomach. They were both enveloped in a shimmering pool of liquid golden light.

Diana felt the light breeze from the jungle pass right through her. Her mind reached out and she understood. She had stepped out of time – pierced the shimmering curtain of golden light Marieji had spoken of so many times. But her life on Gaia was about to come to an ugly end – a sword through her gut.

Are there any options? The question seemed vaguely familiar. She felt strangely calm, somehow totally detached. She scrutinized the swordmaster's body. He was twisted just a bit too much at the waist. *Slightly off balance?* Her eyes dropped to his feet. His stance appeared a bit wide.

There might be one option–

The pool of energy she stood in began to waver like heat waves rising off a metal surface in the mid summer sun. The far away sound of a jet passing overhead rumbled through the back of her mind.

No jets here on Gaia, she realized.

She saw his eyelids begin to fall ever so slowly.

A blink.

Diana felt the pull of a tremendous vacuum. The hair on her arms stood erect, then she heard the roar of a rapidly descending wave of energy.

The envelope of suspended time was closing.

The sense of space between her cells wavered and began to collapse inward. She felt an ancient memory settle into her mind. She would have the advantage of a fraction of a second just as time caught up. *Perhaps…*

The swordmaster's eyelids began to rise ever so slowly from the blink. The tip of his blade inched closer to her unprotected stomach.

Now!

Diana flipped her hand free from the hilt of her sword and dove for Yorrow's feet.

They crashed down together hard onto the packed sand, arms and legs tangled, blades flying wildly.

"Hey." Yarrow sat up in the sand, sputtered, and rubbed the back of his neck. "What in the…was that all about?"

Diana shook her head to clear her mind. She put her hand to her stomach. No blood – only a tiny scratch on the back of her hand. His blade hadn't hit her stomach.

"Did you do what I think you did?" he snapped.

"What?" She stared at the fine line of blood on her hand.

Yarrow eyed her speculatively. "Did you step out of time just then?"

"I don't know, Yarrow. I think I might have," Diana said, incredulous.

"That's it." He jerked himself to his feet and roughly brushed the sand off his bare legs. "No more for you today. Somebody could get hurt with you out of control – jumping around in time like that."

She pulled herself to her feet and glared at him. "Out of control? You were about to disembowel me."

"I would have stopped before I struck you."

"You were off balance."

"Hah," he snorted. "You better go see Marieji. She won't like this. You're supposed to practice being focused, my dear. Not dancing around in time."

Diana picked up her sword and spun to face him. "Don't call me dear," she snapped.

"Oh my." He shook in simulated fear. "The lady warrior shows her true colors."

Diana jammed the blade into her scabbard, turned away without answering, and stomped toward the path to Marieji's hut.

A note by the door read: "At the river."

* * * * *

Diana spotted Marieji at one of her favorite places on the opposite side of the river – back to a rock, eyes closed, and face lifted to the sun. About to call out, she decided instead to honor the other woman's meditation.

She settled down onto the sand. *What happened back there*, she asked herself. *Yorrow is getting really abrupt, almost hostile. Is he right? Am I losing control?*

Diana woke on the sand and grabbed for her sword, but discovered Marieji's foot firmly planted on the scabbard.

Marieji laughed, smoothed a place in the sand with her hand, and settled down lightly next to her. "Why aren't you with Yorrow?"

"He said I should come see you."

"About?"

"Marieji, I think I stepped out of time."

Marieji picked up a small twig, studied it intently. "What makes you think so?" she asked without looking up.

"Yarrow was off balance. He was about to thrust his sword right into my gut and I–"

"Oh? You actually felt Yorrow was off balance? And what happened?"

"Marieji. There was this awful sound…and I felt like my whole body just blow apart on a cellular level. Then this light came – it was like liquid gold. And for a while everything was frozen – nothing moved at all."

"Did you see yourself?"

"What do you mean, see myself? I was right there Marieji. His sword was right at my stomach and–"

Marieji chuckled softly.

"Listen Marieji, it was as though I was standing to the side of both of us. I was frozen just like he was, but I could see everything that was happening."

"Did you see the body you were standing in, Diana?"

"I told you, I was standing right there and…" She fell silent, looked into Marieji's intense eyes.

"Diana, the golden light can only be seen when you let go of your ego self. You didn't see the body you were standing in because you didn't know how to recognize it. You looked out through the eyes of your true center – the pure energy field that materializes your physical body around it. How do you think you accomplished this great feat?"

Diana drew in a slow breath, turned toward the river, blew out her breath with a deep sigh. "I don't know. Maybe because

I knew I was about to be stuck right through. But if I stepped out of my body, what kept me together? Why didn't my body just fall apart?"

"If you had more practice looking, you would have seen that the shimmering golden energy also surrounded your physical body. What you did was step outside your limited ego perceptions of time and space."

"Gads Marieji, how did I do that?"

"You were concerned about your own survival – so were deeply motivated to move your time-space focal point. Your great quantum scientists are telling you that time and space are a continuum – any change in one alters the other. You just slipped outside of your normal place in the continuum."

"But how?"

"The same way you came here to Gaia. You transferred the core of your consciousness, but this time into a much higher frequency vibration."

"But, where did that higher frequency vibration come from?"

"Diana, I've already told you that the core of your being has many frequency bands. You can see the truth of this on a very practical level. Look at your brainwaves, for example. They measure from less than a single cycle per second, all the way into thousands of cycles per second – too fast for your machines to measure."

"And–"

Marieji held up the index finger of her right hand.

Diana had learned to respect the signal as a command for focused attention. She took a deep breath, dropped her shoulders, and slowed her breathing.

Marieji nodded satisfaction. "Diana," she continued, "all you did was focus your consciousness into one of those higher vibratory bands. This allowed you to see from outside the normal limits of your physical body, which vibrates at a much slower level."

"Marieji. I want to do that again. Can I?"

"Of course. Anytime you want to experience such an acceleration of your being, just throw yourself into a situation that brings up deeply intense feelings. But for now, you've forgotten your primary goal. You've got to focus on holding your attention in the moment. Until you accomplish this Diana, nothing else will really serve you."

Diana dug the fingers of her right hand into the sand. The pressure of the sand hurt her knuckles where she had smashed them against the corral rail a few days earlier. She pulled a small stone up out of the sand, examined it closely. *Seems like no matter what, I'm clearly in over my head,* she thought.

Marieji clapped her hands and chuckled. "OK, I can see you're definitely ready to step more consciously into the fabric of life – to experience the oneness of all things. It's time for a vision quest."

Diana stared at Marieji. "Vision quest. Marieji, what do you mean? Go out into the wilderness by myself like some wild creature? Why would I do that? I've already got enough challenges."

Marieji laughed her deep, rolling laugh. "Diana, this is an ancient way of seeking personal power – a tradition found in almost every culture, all the way back in time."

"But what's to be gained from going out in the wilderness alone like that? Come on, Marieji. Can't you be reasonable?"

"You're ready for a deeper experience of your relationship to the rest of nature, Diana. From this you'll be better able to create the meaning of your life."

Diana again dug her fingers into the sand, extracted another pebble, placed it thoughtfully next to the first, then dug for yet another. She felt deeply restless. *Meaning of my life? How*, she wondered, *will I ever find that?*

Silence.

Diana shook her head. "You know Marieji. When I think of the meaning of my life, I'm not so certain I want to return to Earth at all. Life seems so much more peaceful here. Earth is one just big ecological war zone. How can life have any meaning at all there?"

"You must try to return."

"It's just so painful, what we've done to the Earth. And Gaia is so…so unspoiled."

"If you manage to return, maybe you'll choose to help turn the tide – put a halt to mankind's abusive ways and put some healing into action.

Diana sighed, dug up another pebble and placed it on the sand. She contemplated Marieji's words. *Maybe time alone on the mountain would help.* "When should I go on this quest?"

"Fast tonight. Go to bed early, and come to the hot springs tomorrow morning at sunrise. I want you to soak before you go up onto the mountain. No sword or food. Just bring a blanket, your knife, and two canteens of water."

ෆ౫ఎ

CHAPTER EIGHTEEN

It's not that life has consciousness.
Life is consciousness.

— Gibrilken

DIANA'S EYES SMARTED from the salt-laden sweat that ran
in a steady stream off her eyebrows, dripping into the corners
of her eyes. The mineral water was so hot she could barely
stand to move her arms and legs.

She peered at Marieji through the thick cloud of steam
rising from the rock-lined hot mineral pool. "But why are you
saying I should force myself to stand on my feet all night,
Marieji? Isn't it enough that I'll be up on that mountain all
alone?"

"The darkness of night is the best time to seek a vision,
Diana. Exhaustion will help dissolve your ego self and open
you to alternate ways of seeing. Plus your shadow self comes
more clearly in the night. And if you're on your feet, you're
more likely to remain awake to talk with her."

"Shadow self?"

"Yes. The part of yourself you've hidden away from the light of day. You can never fully stand in power until you embrace this part of your being."

"That sounds creepy. And if this part of myself is hidden so deep Marieji, how will I recognize it anyway?"

"You'll recognize it by your fear. Fear is what caused you to hide that part of yourself away to begin with. So when you feel fear rise up within you, look for your shadow self. You'll likely find her standing just behind you."

"Great. So then what?"

Marieji signaled for her to step out of the water. "Now into the cold pool."

Diana submerged herself into the pool, gasped and immediately catapulted up out of the frigid water

Marieji pointed at the pool. "Back in," she laughed.

"So what do I do about this...this shadow self?"

"You need to call her out, Diana – ask her to stand with you and think together into the one mind."

"The one mind?" Diana chattered, now up to her neck in the frigid water. "You mean my conscious mind?"

"No. Your individual mind is only a small part of the one mind. Remember, the very nature of life is consciousness. Our individual minds just reach into that great source of our consciousness – the one mind."

Diana knitted her brow and stared at Marieji in intense silence. *Will it ever be possible to understand what she's talking about?* "Are you referring to God, Marieji?"

"Some might choose to call it that. The one mind contains

all consciousness – understands, knows and remembers everything. There is no place it is not. And so…the same conscious force that grows mighty mountains from the molten center of the earth, also grows each thought in your mind."

"How is my brain part of this?"

"Your personal physical brain is a bio-energetic sending and receiving set that thinks into the one mind, Diana."

Diana rose up out of the frigid water, teeth chattering. She wrapped her arms around her chest and picked her way gingerly across the rocks to stand in the warmth of the sun. The earth s shifted beneath the soles of her feet. *An earthquake?*

Marieji looked straight into her, giving no indication that anything unusual had occurred.

"Here are your instructions," Marieji said once Diana had dried herself in the sun. "Go to the very top of the mountain and find your place. Mark the limits of where you will take your stand. You can use rocks, a line drawn in the sand – whatever you wish."

Diana nodded.

"Now listen to me carefully. Your body contains the memories of all of your ancestors – all the way back to tribal times. Those memories are woven into the strands of your DNA in every cell of your being. So trust your intuition. When the moon rises, stand to greet her. Remain standing until the sun rises." Marieji hesitated, gazed deeply at Diana.

Diana met her gaze.

"While the sun is out," she continued, "sit in meditation.

Try not to give your power away to tiredness or fear. Don't stand in judgment of what comes to you. I'll wait for you here."

Diana opened her mouth to speak, but Marieji held up her hand for silence.

"Diana, return to this place by mid-day, two days from today."

* * * * *

Diana stopped for a drink at a small spring. The trees were getting smaller, more sparse, the higher she climbed. She topped off her canteens, tied them back to her belt, shifted the rolled blanket to her other shoulder, then looked up at the barren mountaintop.

She contemplated how she felt more and more connected to Gaia, to the way of life and values, to the unspoiled beauty of the jungle environment.

I should be searching for a way to stay here, rather than how to return to my old life, she thought. She looked down at her tanned, newly muscled arms and legs. Gaia was in her veins, she felt at one with this world.

Could I have a place here? Is it possible?

She shook herself and held up her fingers to judge the remaining distance as Marieji had taught her. She still had at least one-third of the way to climb, and the sun was already approaching its peak. She had to stay focused.

* * * * *

The evergreen trees gave way to spindly shoulder high red barked Manzanita bushes, clumps of dried grass, and lichen covered rocks. Above was the peak, and nothing but barren rocks. She realized she wouldn't find firewood on the top of the mountain.

Diana shook open her blanket, snapped the dried branches off a few gray-barked dead Manzanita and piled them into her blanket. Satisfied with her collection of firewood, she shouldered the load and set out straight toward the peak.

She found herself walking over treacherous gravel in a barren environment of wind-rounded boulders and sparse patches of crusty gray-green lichen.

* * * * *

The sunlight felt different on the mountaintop – searing, totally dry, deeply penetrating. Diana used her newly found skill of welcoming nature and accepted the heat bouncing off the mountaintop into herself, rather than trying to repel it.

She shielded her eyes and looked out over the lush jungle stretching out from the bottom of the mountain to the south, then turned to the west and scanned the horizon.

The dragon's peak was easy to spot – the highest point of the western mountain range. She surveyed the broad area between the jungle and the dragon's peak – it wavered with intense heat reflecting off the parched sand she had learned was common to Gaia's badlands.

She turned slowly in a circle to find a place to make camp. A particular flat spot attracted her. Diana stepped onto the spot and again slowly turned in a circle. Three directions were unobstructed. She would be able to clearly see the sunrise, the sunset and the dragon's peak, yet have a large boulder to her back.

She emptied her firewood, wrapped the canteens in her blanket and placed it atop the large boulder, then squatted on her haunches to survey her site.

Something doesn't feel right, she thought. *What did Marieji say? Oh yes. "My body contains the memory of all of my ancestors, all the way back to tribal times."*

"OK," she announced out loud. "I definitely want a circle. I feel naked and exposed up here all by myself."

Diana selected a flat rock and began to scrape away the smaller rocks and gravel until she revealed the underlying granite-hard soil.

By late afternoon she had cleared a circle about twelve feet across, and had placed several small piles of stones around the entire perimeter.

She stood and admired her work, then knelt in the center of the circle and began to scrape the area flat using a hand-sized shard of black rock. Once satisfied, she lowered herself onto her hands and knees and blew the center clean.

As a final touch, she dug a small hole for the collection of sun-bleached bones she had found in a tiny abandoned bird nest. She marked the site with a pile of stones.

The sun hung suspended just above the dragon's peak as she arranged kindling in her rock fire pit. Diana folded her blanket, placed it in the flat spot in the center of the circle, and settled down to contemplate the sunset. She defocused her eyes as Marieji had taught her, allowing herself to merge with the setting sun.

The top of the dragon's peak glowed like a candle long after the sun had dropped below the horizon – almost as though lighted from within.

* * * * *

As twilight deepened, Diana rose to her feet and began to pace restlessly around the limits of her circle. Finally she stopped to contemplate an especially bright star that had appeared low in the eastern horizon.

The memory of standing with her great aunt outside her summer tent at the lake, looking up to make a wish on the first star of the evening, flooded into her memory.

Diana recalled that it was she who had introduced her to the joy of being outdoors. Who had taken her to the lake when she was yet a very young child. Who had taught her to pick wild blueberries and sing old songs around the evening campfire – *"Froggie went a courting he did ride. Um hum. Um hum. Froggie went a courting he did ride, with a rifle and a pistol by his side..."*

She raised her arms upward toward the bright star. "I honor your memory." *Everyone thought you were a bit loony because you talked to the birds,* she thought. *But you know, I think I remember the birds answering you. I'm sure I do. I truly wish I'd gotten to know you better.*

The night was very still.

Diana wrapped herself in her blanket, paced, and fought the impulse to curl up next to the fire.

Finally the first tip of the full moon appeared above the eastern horizon, easing the dark tension on the peak. Down in the valley the wild dogs began to howl, and the deep hoots of the great night birds floated up the mountainside.

Diana faced the moon as she had been instructed, but shivered and shifted back and forth from one foot to the other – restless and unsettled. Feelings of loneliness and sadness crept into the back of her mind

A primitive sense of abandonment finally settled over her. It felt ancient, unexplainable, and deeply disturbing.

As the night deepened her shivering progressed into a constant, bone-rattling shudder. She added wood to the fire, then wrapped the blanket tighter around herself, pulling a portion up over her head. Her leg muscles quivered with exhaustion.

"I must be totally nuts," she muttered. "The only thing I'm really learning from this is to avoid going up on a mountaintop alone at night. Oh brother! Where *is* the sun?"

* * * * *

It had been a long night. As the eastern sky finally began to lighten, Diana sank down with exhausted relief next to the fire, then began to drift in and out of a trance-like state.

She felt weightless, and had the sensation of floating in warm water. An odd sound played through her mind. As the sound moved faster and faster her feet began to tingle, then vibrate. Diana burrowed deeper into her blanket.

The vibration traveled up her legs to her lower back, then erupted in tiny spasms until her entire body began to convulse in rhythmical waves.

She was too exhausted to resist. A pattern of bright lights flashed behind her closed eyelids. *Feels almost like I'm flying*, she thought.

Then she opened her eyes and discovered herself in the air, flying high above the barren mountaintop.

An odd circle of rocks caught her attention. There was someone stretched out down there. *A human?* Diana gasped as she recognized herself hundreds of feet below.

In the next instant she found herself back in her body, unable to move. Waves of warm ecstasy flowed up from her feet all the way into the very top of her head.

* * * * *

When the first sliver of sunlight streaked across the crisp morning sky, she finally felt rested enough to sit up.

She spent the morning in a daze – searching for some logical answer to her ultra-real sensation of flying far above the mountaintop.

Although early afternoon found even exhaustion setting in, Diana realized she needed more firewood. She forced herself onto her feet and hiked back down to gather another blanket-full of dry sticks.

By the time she reached her campsite on the top of the mountain, the heat was unbearable. She propped the three longest sticks up against the boulder, then stretched her blanket over them to make a rough shelter from the sun. She collapsed in her make-shift shade and lost herself to deep meditation throughout the intense afternoon heat.

The shrill cry of a Gaia hawk suddenly startled her into full awareness. It was late afternoon and she was stiff, thirsty and hungry. She searched the sky in all directions, but couldn't find the hawk.

Again and again throughout the late afternoon she heard the distinct cry of the bird, but each time was unable to spot it in the sky.

CৠৎO

CHAPTER NINETEEN

A man's spiritual consciousness is not awakened
until his Kundalini is aroused.

—Sri Ramakrishna (1836-1886)

THE HAWK'S CRY rang out again just as Diana settled onto her
blanket to face into the sunset. She turned to search the sky, but
the bird was nowhere to be seen. An oddly familiar sensation
that seemed just out of reach of her conscious mind crept up
her spine. Her scalp tingled. Diana shook it off and forced
herself to focus on the sunset.

The entire western sky was streaked with flaming bands
of umber, bright orange, salmon and deep red. The sky directly
above her vibrated with muted bands of pink and violet. Even
the barren mountaintop itself was radiant with a soft, luminous
glow.

She suddenly realized that she seemed to have unusual
visual clarity. The reflection of the sunset off the wind-worn

surfaces of the mountaintop had added deep accents to the lines and edges of the rocks.

Almost like a painting, she thought. *Just too beautiful.*

As the sky darkened she stood and turned slowly in a circle. Moisture had gathered in the sky to the north. Delicate fingers of pink and gray clouds reached across the sky toward her mountaintop retreat.

* * * * *

The early evening wind was a knife of ice and the fire offered little relief. Diana wrapped the blanket even tighter around herself, but the wind sliced right through it.

Shivering, she took her stance to wait for the moonrise. She was surprised to find that in spite of the cold, she easily settled into a deep meditative state.

She let her mind merge with the cold wind, and had the feeling she had so welcomed it before – perhaps in another lifetime? A brief memory of being a male Viking standing on a barren cliff looking out over the sea flashed through her mind. The vision passed and Diana quietly watched the entire valley disappear beneath a cover of thick gray fog.

Her meditation was interrupted by an intense blast of icy wind that scattered sparks in all directions. She realized she would either have to leave the circle, or put the fire out. Unwilling to go without the comfort of a fire, she pushed the coals together and added more wood, then moved out of the circle and took her stance on the very peak of the mountain.

She defocused her eyes to take in the full vista of the

moonlit blanket of fog that now totally shrouded the valley in all directions.

Time stretched out. Diana spaced in and out of conscious thought until an especially strong gust of the frigid wind sent her staggering. She clutched her blanket tighter and leaned into the wind. Thick fingers of fog began to swirl around her feet.

The entire mountaintop quickly disappeared as a sky full of fog and heavy-bellied storm clouds swallowed the full moon. She found herself totally surrounded by impenetrable fog below, and heavy storm clouds above.

There was no land or sky to be seen.

The hawk's cry cut through the howl of the wind.

"No way," she cried out. "Not a hawk. Not here, and most certainly not at night in this weather. Even I know that's totally impossible."

Her flesh prickled. Someone, or something, was standing directly behind her. Diana dropped into the warrior's stance and spun around.

There was no one there.

She struggled against increasingly rubbery knees, tried unsuccessfully to stop her teeth from chattering.

Again she felt the presence.

This time as she spun around she saw a dark shimmering outline of something, someone, just out of reach.

"I know who you are," she shouted. Diana gulped back an impulse to scream and run. *Run where?* The mountaintop was totally gone. She stood suspended in an envelope of thick fog and thunder clouds.

Again she clearly felt the presence just behind her. Her heart thundered against her ribs.

"I call you out to stand with me," she shouted through chattering teeth.

Only the wind answered – howling around her in a tighter and tighter circle.

The cry of the hawk came again from somewhere out over the valley.

Diana felt an odd pressure just behind her shoulder blades, then a hot tingling in her solar plexus. Then her jaw dropped as a clear ray of shimmering light burst forth from her gut.

She looked out over the shaft of light.

It connected to what looked like a grid of energy stretching out over the entire landscape. Each node of the grid glowed with the same golden light, some nodes more brightly than others. She was directly connected to the grid by the ray of light that had burst forth from her solar plexus.

Her head spun. A tingling sensation streamed up her spine and pulsated at the top of her head.

Diana pulled one hand out of the blanket to rub an intensely hot, prickly area just above the bridge of her nose.

Suddenly she realized that she was actually seeing the grid from top, bottom and all sides – simultaneously.

The air around her glowed even brighter. It seemed as though everything had been coated with liquid gold. She tried to blink it away, then realized that the golden gridwork crisscrossed virtually everything – it was both outside of her, and included her.

A sense of great familiarity and knowing settled over her.

There are no words to describe this, she realized. *I have always known…have always been here.*

The distinct flapping of large wings cut through the howl of the wind. The hawk cried to her, then called to her yet again.

Her body became extremely light as she reached out to the bird and began to float along her spoke of light out over the grid. But the instant she realized that her feet were no longer touching a solid surface, she was overcome by deep shock.

She collapsed to the ground as though she had dropped several feet from out of a vacuum.

The golden web was gone.

She was left only with the shadow of an oddly luminous figure that pressed down even closer to her, yet was somehow out of reach. She struggled against her fear. Then one intense spasm after another began to explode from the base of her spine and light up the inside of her skull with strange lights.

She heard the hawk and cried out to it.

The only answer was the heart-rending howl of the wind as it tore across the barren mountaintop.

* * * * *

Diana woke in her circle to an ultra-bright, crisp morning sun – her blanket still gripped tightly around her.

Except for a light wind, the morning was silent.

She immediately noticed that the large boulder at her back somehow seemed alive in the early sunlight, as though it had a personal history and life all its own.

"Maybe it does," she pondered. "I remember Marieji telling me that the very nature of life – all forms of life – is consciousness. I think I see what she means."

She placed both hands on the boulder. "Thank you for protecting my back," she said. She was startled to notice what felt like a vibration coming from out of the rock.

Diana scooped up the remaining cold ashes from her fire and threw them into the wind, then scattered the small piles of rocks she had placed to mark her circle.

She had just tied the empty canteens to her belt and shouldered her blanket roll when the hawk cried out yet again. A warm excitement and resolve swelled into her. She and the hawk were connected – everything was connected.

* * * * *

The hawk cried to her several times as she walked back down the mountain.

Her mind swayed back and forth between feelings of overpowering joy and nagging unrest. Several times she looked over her shoulder to see if she was being followed.

CRSO

CHAPTER TWENTY

Man did not weave the web of life.
He is merely a strand in it. But whatever
he does to the web, he does to himself.

—Attributed to Chief Pontiac

MARIEJI ROSE TO greet her, held out her hands for the
blanket and canteens. "Into the hot spring," she said. "Relax
and I'll drum for you."

Diana threw off her shoes and clothes and sighed with
relief as she eased her body into the shady end of the steaming
mineral pool. The hot water immediately began to work its way
into the exhausted muscles of her legs and back. She felt her
shoulders sink and her stomach relax. *I could sit here all day,*
she thought. *All day and into the night…and maybe forever.*

Marieji gently lifted her drum from a berry-stained leather
cover and held it up to the sun to tighten the drumskin.
"I've decided to drum the history of Gaia for you Diana – in

honor of your vision quest." She slid her hands over the tight skin, caressing, tapping lightly, coaxing and teasing the drum into life.

Diana sank deeper into the steaming pool of mineral water. Brief snapshots of her experience the night before slid through her mind. *What was that golden grid? And that shimmering shadow? Was it the shadow self Marieji mentioned?*

Marieji began to chant in a language that Diana had never before heard her use. The words were melodic, lilting, and somehow vaguely familiar.

Vivid images leapt into Diana's mind. The drum and chant painted clear mental pictures of a clean, warm, light rain and a steaming forest mist. Of long stretches of valleys with rich fertile loam and wide rivers. Of vast mountain ranges spread thick with forests of giant trees, their bark the color of the coka nut, and water that thundered down sparkling waterfalls through all the seasons of the year.

She saw clear images of high alpine meadows painted with rainbows of waist-high wild flowers. Hidden springs and plentiful fresh, clean water. Pristine polar caps with sharp edges and icy winds blowing fresh air into high currents that spread around all the planet. And a peaceful people who lived close to, and deeply loved, the land.

Marieji's eyes glittered in the sunlight and her body swayed with the rhythm of the drum. Then suddenly the muscles of her neck tightened. The intensity of the rhythm began to build.

The drum, the chant, spoke clearly of what had come to the land. Diana was there. She shuddered as she saw huge machines belch clouds of foul, black exhaust. As deafening noise tore into the jungle and the sky darkened with clouds of smoke from the merciless fires that followed. Her heart shredded as she saw tribes of gentle people turned out from the homes of their ancestors to wander out into the newly-created wastelands and starve – their very souls shattered beyond repair.

She saw the wild creatures scatter through the land sick and dying. Many had been slaughtered aimlessly – their feet made into ashtrays, their proud heads hung on the walls of the aggressors' sterile homes. Their bodies were simply left behind to rot in the sun.

Then once they had stripped away the lush vegetation, the aggressors threw out grass seed to create grazing lands for the steroid-drugged animals they raised to supply their craving for the adrenaline-filled flesh of innocent creatures fully aware they were about to be slaughtered.

The grazing animals quickly exhausted the grass. The aggressors moved on, ripping up yet more of the great rain forest to create new grazing lands. A featureless, barren desert wasteland followed closely in their wake.

The once lush jungle was soon limited to a few remote areas surrounded by high mountains. Then flying machines began to circle over even those areas as the aggressors plotted how to best claim the last remaining ancient resources.

The rhythm of the drum changed. Diana found herself sitting with a small group of people of many different skin colors. They had gathered deep in the heart of one of the few remaining areas of forested jungle.

They shared a common intent.

The firelight gleamed in their eyes.

Diana saw and shared the fear and passion and absolute determination reflected in those eyes. With soulful intent she sat with them, was one with them as they wrapped their energies together into a huge vortex of energy that extended out to the very edges of the small patch of remote jungle.

Joining together in a booming hymn of praise, they raised a soulful appeal to the very heart of the planet. They asked her for rain – rain of an intensity to make the jungle impenetrable, to render the aggressors' machines inoperable.

She felt her heart burst as the sky opened and the great rains began. They continued their song for a month – until the sides of the mountain fell away in the torrents of water.

Their refuge fell into isolation, totally worthless to the aggressors.

They had taken the jungle into themselves.

The drum then spoke of the conscious, intentional community that had evolved. They taught their children to walk lightly on nature, to care for her as they would their own bodies.

They and their world were one.

The drum fell off into a fertile silence.

"How do you feel?" Marieji asked as Diana stepped out of the hot spring.

"Different. As though…" She searched within herself for the words to express the limitless feeling of well-being flowing through her. "As though I'm all new inside. Does that make any sense, Marieji?"

Marieji nodded agreement, then swept her hand over the bread and fruit she had arranged on a woven mat.

"Hungry?"

Diana ate in silent gratitude for the raw beauty of the fruit and bread. Each bite was an entirely new experience of ecstasy. The scent of the jungle and the hot spring rose around her rich and alive. She felt her heart move out to embrace even the tiny ant that had crawled up onto her leg.

She crumbled a bit of her bread and placed it in a small pile next to an ant trail, gently encouraged the ant off her leg and onto a leaf, then placed the leaf next to her offering.

Marieji smiled knowingly. "Diana, you said earlier that you felt as though you had flown through the air like a hawk. Did the bird have a red tail?"

Diana nodded.

"Interesting. Many of your Native Americans believe that the red-tailed hawk is a powerful symbol of transformation – that it signals the awakening of clear vision, and perhaps the initiation of a visionary life purpose."

"Visionary?"

"Yes. Tell me everything you saw before you returned to your body."

Diana surprised herself as she recounted something she hadn't consciously recalled seeing from the air. It was a vision of a blue-green planet – its once great coastal cities totally buried beneath a huge ocean. The inland villages were also deserted – mere piles of rubble in the midst of barren wastelands. The only signs of life had been a few small settlements scattered through the mountain forests.

"One possible near future of Earth," Marieji sighed.

Diana had known even before Marieji confirmed her fears. She had sensed the truth on a deep, undeniable level.

"What can be done, Marieji? Is there anything?"

"Oh yes, indeed. But that something will have to spring forth from the hearts and determination of the people. No government will be able to deal successfully with the Great Change."

"Great Change. Didn't you tell me that was the beginning of Gaia? That it started just before the end of the millennium? That we would–"

"Yes to all of your questions, Diana."

Diana shook her head sadly. She recalled reading an interpretation of the quatrains of Nostradamus – how he had predicted back in the 16th century that the last few years before and just after the year 2000 would be marked by overwhelming social upheavals and immense Earth changes.

Is it really happening? She asked herself. *Is that what the increasing earthquakes on the Pacific Rim are all about? All the recent floods in the United States and the ice storms across Europe?* "So," Diana said softly. "I assume it's going to be everyone for themselves during this Great Change."

Marieji sat silently, laid her hand on the drum, then looked up at her with peaceful eyes. "Not at all, Diana. There is a higher path. One that you yourself may choose to walk – if you successfully return to Earth, that is."

Diana held her gaze. She followed the older woman's example – breathed gently and slowly, sank her awareness down deep into herself, waited.

Marieji finally nodded her head as though she had settled a deeply intense internal debate. "All right, Diana. I'll share my understanding with you. You saw into a great truth of life on that mountaintop. Each of us is connected to the great web – the one source of life. You and I are each a node on that web. In essence, we are all one interconnected being." She paused and laughed as an iridescent green beetle suddenly buzzed right past her nose.

Diana felt as though she had heard that laugh for the first time. The sound rose up out of Marieji deep, rich and full. She looked closely at the older woman, noticed for the first time the scar on her forehead above the right brow. Noted even her scent – like the spicy vanilla incense she burned in her hut.

A sense of deep love flowed through Diana. *Everything seems so clear. So different,* she thought. She wondered why she'd never noticed these things before, then realized that she had, deep down inside herself. Tears began to flow down her cheeks. She made no attempt to dry them.

"Some of the nodes are brighter than others, Marieji. I felt as though they held more energy."

The same energy is available to all of us, Marieji thought in reply, without speaking the words.

Diana gasped. It was always such a surprise to hear the other woman's thoughts so clearly in her own mind. She laughed. "Marieji, it's all so beautiful. There are no words–"

"Diana, the web you saw is all of life itself – the great creative force. Each node is a ray of consciousness belonging to one particular being. We are truly connected to one another

– and to the great creative force."

Diana sat in silent rapture, listened.

"The web extends through all the worlds to infinity. Great shamans and masters of consciousness often travel the web. They can disassemble and reassemble their body on any of the different dimensions of a world at will. The rest of us generally assemble our beings in only one dimension at a time."

"How do they do that?"

"It all goes back to vibration, Diana. To see into another dimension, and especially to manifest yourself fully there, you must be able to change the level of vibration of your being to match the vibratory level of that dimension. To hear in another dimension, for example, you must retune your ear to recognize and interpret sound waves moving at a different frequency than those your physical ear is normally able to hear."

"But what does that have to do with the Great Change?"

"Some say the Earth herself is preparing to manifest herself on a higher vibratory level – that the Great Change is actually the Phoenix in early stages of awakening. As the Phoenix arises, those who manage to move with Earth into her higher vibratory level will see her in an entirely new light. While those who remain locked into the old vibratory level will see only violence and destruction."

"Phew, Marieji, how can I learn to hold that new level of vibration?"

"For now just focus on the path of the warrior – learn to be totally present and open to the moment. Earth's mental institutions are full of people who can hear and see into several dimensions, but can't manage to hold their focus steadily in any one of them."

"What an insight," Diana exclaimed.

"Clear focus comes first," Marieji continued. "Then you must learn to passionately create, and fully become, the meaning of your life. Such a passionate commitment will automatically move your entire being into higher frequency vibrations."

They sat for some time in silence.

Create meaning in my life? Diana knew she hadn't done that – had never come close. Life had just come as it had come, and meaning had always seemed somehow just out of reach. "Marieji," she said softly. "I don't think I really understand what you mean by 'creating' the meaning of my life. I've searched most of my life, but I've never managed to find the meaning of life."

"Meaning is not something you find, Diana. As I said, you create meaning."

"Well if that's the case, then I'm not much of a creator."

"Perhaps not just yet Diana. But do you think a great artist is able to create perfectly without practice? To simply walk up to a canvas and create a great masterpiece that matches her vision perfectly the first time?"

"No, of course not."

"Creating the meaning of your life is no different. The secret is to start by first determining what's important to you. Then you develop that into a clear vision, and manifest it into being. Your first result won't match your vision perfectly. So you create and adjust. Creating meaning is a process, not a goal. And the concept of failure doesn't apply – not at all

Each step absolutely takes you closer to your meaning."

They sat again in silence.

Marieji broke the silence. "Would you like to look for some possible sources of your meaning?"

Diana threw a handful of bread crumbs onto the sand next to the stream. "Of course," she said quietly.

"Sit comfortably."

Diana crossed her legs and rested her hands in her lap, allowed her eyes to defocus gently, took a deep breath, and let her consciousness follow her breath all the way down into her belly. She smiled, recalling how difficult this had been in the beginning. *The beginning–*

Good.

She had again heard Marieji think directly to her mind-to-mind. She took another deep breath and felt her body begin to stretch out, become very light and elongated. The sounds of the jungle drifted farther and farther away – echoed to her as though down a long corridor.

Diana? Marieji thought to her.

Yes? She thought back.

Remain here with me. Just keep your eyes closed, and share with me images of what you have loved the most in your life. Things which have been easy and effortless and wonderful for you.

Diana pulled a deep, satisfying breath down into the bottom of her lungs. The first image began to form.

She was in an ancient redwood forest…breathing deeply, walking along a steam winding down through a valley in the coastal mountain range behind California's Monterey Bay. The scent of the redwoods was rich in the summer air. She removed her boots and sox and waded into the cool stream.

The image changed abruptly. She sat with an intimate group of friends around a fire, laughing. It was the best of warm, loving companionship.

She sighed, then found herself out in her grandparents' garden. Warm sunshine fell on her hair and arms. The scent of lavender and fresh strawberries filled the air. Her grandmother's sweet high soprano voice called to her.

Diana's heart swelled to bursting as the scene changed yet again. She was on her knees in her best friend's backyard. The freshly cut grass was damp through the knees of her jeans. Her friend's first son, about three years old, was with her, playing together with the family's new calico kitten.

"Diana." Marieji called her out of her reverie.

She opened her eyes. Hot tears streamed down her cheeks.

"Diana, I have seen your visions. You have a deep love of nature, loving companionship, and the creatures of Earth. Is that true?"

"Oh yes, I really do."

"So where else would you look for the meaning of your life?"

"But Marieji, what do those things have to do with the meaning of life? Isn't the meaning of life supposed to be something deeply metaphysical or spiritual?"

"Diana, everything you do is totally spiritual. Do you think your spirit goes away just because you're digging a ditch. How could spirit *not* be involved? And where would it go?"

"Still, I always thought the meaning of life was something I had to search for."

"Not search for – create. And powerful meaning can only be created by working with what you are truly passionate about, what really matters to you. Where else would you start? You have to be in love with something for it to have any meaning at all for you. And if you can't be passionate and deeply enthusiastic about what you've chosen to do, why bother with it at all?"

Diana opened her mouth to ask another question, but remained silent when Marieji lifted her hand with one finger pointed upward – her signal for attention.

"Diana, you will never be truly successful or happy doing something that requires efforting. Seek out that which you love, then pour your energy into it. Only then can you truly make your life a sacred experience and find real meaning on a deep level. Anyway, how can you assume that the deep love you feel for the Earth and other beings is mundane?"

"But how can such simple things bring any meaning to my life? And Marieji, it's not like I can make a living doing them."

"Isn't that an interesting assumption? Who inside of you says that? It sounds as though someone in your life taught you that your life's work had to be laborious – something to do not because you love it, but just to earn money. Is that so?"

"Well of course, Marieji."

"So you were expected to grow out of your childhood self indulgence and come suffer along with them. True?"

Diana nodded agreement.

"Did you see them happy in their efforting?"

"No, and neither was I." She shook off the black cloud associated with turning from her love of sculpture to instead make a living as a commercial graphic artist. Just for money. The pain of it had haunted her for years.

Why did you do that, Diana? Marieji thought to her.

"I had to make a living. But all I ended up doing was working to pay my bills…so I could work and pay more bills," Diana sighed. "There was no meaning to my life all."

"So where was your passion, your enthusiasm?"

"Passion? Are you kidding?"

Marieji quietly looked into Diana's eyes. "Well," she said. "There is really one basic meaning to life. You are alive for the purpose of your soul's evolution and growth. You are the one mind, the great creative force, playing at being Diana. Perhaps you should look to what you love…then from there you can create more satisfaction and joy in your life."

That does make sense, Diana thought.

"Like every other human being Diana, you possess a totally unique blend of talents and potentials. You are like no one else. And since you will only be successful at what you love anyway, why not just turn your search in that direction?"

"That sounds almost too…too easy," Diana sighed.

"That may be why so many pass it by. But what do you have to lose except your unhappiness and frustration?"

Diana shook her head. "It really is simple, isn't it?"

A simple truth, but an extremely difficult lesson, Marieji thought to her.

They walked in silence back to the village.

"Diana," Marieji said as they reached the porch. "From now on you should keep your sword with you at all times – even when sleeping. You've opened the door to a very powerful new realm, and that door swings both ways."

The unspoken message behind Marieji's words sliced along her spine like a sharp blade.

CHAPTER TWENTY ONE

Make inner freedom your primary goal in life.

—*J. Donald Walters*

DIANA WOKE AND found herself in the grips of a silence and darkness so deep it could only be death.

"Am I dead?" she asked herself in the blackness.

Silence.

Then, as if though from far away, she heard the echo of a man's voice.

"OK, White," the voice said coldly. "We'll give you a chance to present your findings at staff this afternoon."

She heard footsteps of several people walking on a hard surface, and many others talking in the background. There was a somehow familiar smell about the place.

A hospital, she realized. *I'm in the hospital.*

Diana forced her eyes open. Through a sickening dizziness she realized she was actually still in bed – in the hut.

I'm in Gaia. Did I visit myself in the hospital on Earth? Diana asked herself. *Most likely.*

She shook herself, climbed out of bed, and went out onto the porch to breath the crisp night air. Her vision had been far too real to be a dream.

* * * * *

Dr. Katie White cleared her throat for the third time. She never found it easy to do a presentation at the Bear's staff meetings. He was like a slab of granite. She slid long sheets of brainwave readings onto the conference table, lifting one so all six residents and Dr. Brennan could view them.

"These are the long-term comas," White began. "You can see that their brainwave activity is very flat and mostly in the extremely low delta range."

She held up the third printout, "This is the Jane Doe admitted with head trauma a little over a week ago. Her activity was very different at this point. I have recordings that look almost like those of a person in a light dreaming sleep."

"What's your interpretation, White?" Brennan asked.

"Well, she's definitely not a typical comatose patient," she explained. "And take a look at this particular reading."

She held up a computer graphic covered with red notes. "This looks a lot like the readings I saw once for a shaman that was—"

"Shaman?" Brennan exploded. "What kind of garbage is this, White? I thought you were conducting a medical experiment."

"I am, Dr. Brennan. It's just that her patterns seem very similar to those of an exceptional class of people. A shaman, for example, can–"

"That's it, White. I don't think we need to hear any more of this black magic crap."

* * * * *

Doug Chaffey removed his stethoscope and bent over the brainwave tracings his fellow resident Katie White had spread the length of the cafeteria table. "Looks like your Jane Doe has gone through some pretty dramatic changes, doesn't it?"

"I think she has, Doug. But look at this from earlier this morning. She was all over the place again. She had spikes all the way up into alpha – the area of the conscious, waking brain. You could swear she was just in a deep sleep, with real active dreams. But just before the staff meeting she went totally flat again. It's almost as though she's slipping further and further away. Strange…"

"See any signs that she's coming out of the coma?"

"Nothing really consistent," She shrugged and folded up the computer printout. "Let's get some lunch."

CHAPTER TWENTY TWO

If we all did the things we are capable of doing,
we would literally astound ourselves.

— *Thomas Edison*

DIANA MOVED ALONG the river path in total darkness, allowing her feet pick the best way over a large root that had grown across the path. She stopped in a pool of moonlight shining through the thick jungle canopy. A pocket bat brushed past her right ear in committed pursuit of a moth.

Three months of Gaia time, she thought. *I can hardly believe I've been here that long – but Marieji says it's only about a week of true Earth time. How strange,* she thought.

A deep sadness welled up within her.

Her fingers went to the dragon's head necklace Marieji had given her two nights before. She had successfully managed to follow Marieji through the jungle in total darkness, and had found her sitting patiently by the river.

Another bat zipped around her head.

"Get present," Diana demanded of herself. She closed her eyes and stepped forward to test her ability to move through the night without using the moonlight.

* * * * *

She circled the hut in the darkness before stepping up onto the porch. Lately Marieji had made sport of traveling ahead of her using her warrior's intent, then leaping out from behind and attacking if her guard was down.

Seems clear. She pulled off her scabbard, laid it on the porch within easy reach, then massaged the tight muscles in her upper back against a bamboo post. *I should go soak in the hot spring tomorrow to loosen these tight muscles,* she thought. "Muscles," Diana chuckled. "If Jeff could see me now, he would never believe this body. "

Wonder if he's even discovered I'm in the hospital, she wondered. *Oh well,* she reminded herself, *from what I've learned lately, it's really time to let go anyway. If I'm going to be in a relationship, it's going to have to be far more honest and fulfilling – not just a rebound.*

She took hold of the post with both hands, positioned her feet at the base, and leaned out into a deep stretch. She held her stretch and inhaled a deep breath of the sweet night-blooming Toua blossoms. The scent reminded her of gardenias.

Intoxicating. She recalled that Marieji had said that the blooms always came just before the spring rains. *Feels like time for the orange trees to blossom.* She thought of her childhood summers in the inland valley. How the evening air hung thick with the sweet scent of orange blossoms on neatly manicured rows of trees stretching all the way up into the foothills.

"Earth. Oh, sweet Earth," she sighed. Her mind rebelled against her vision of the current truth. The orchards were gone. The trees had been torn up by the roots and burned – replaced by endless concrete, asphalt, stucco and glass. The rain no longer fell onto the soil. Now it fell onto asphalt streets and parking lots diverting their precious cargo into coldly impersonal concrete storm drains that dumped it into the ocean. Nature no longer comfortably lived in the Earth of her California childhood.

Diana pulled aside the door net and stepped into the hut. Chat Chew had already claimed her spot at the foot of the bed. She undressed, slid her scabbard beneath the bed, kissed the top of the cat's head, and crawled under the blanket.

* * * * *

In her dream Diana heard the hawk cry out to her. She answered, and immediately found herself in flight.

A blue-green landscape stretched far beneath her. She flew down through the thick clouds and found herself over a vaguely familiar mountain range. The highest peak had been blown away – replaced by a deep crater from a recent volcanic eruption.

Three smaller peaks leaked clouds of noxious gas and steady ribbons of molten lava.

Long-cooled rivers of porous lava wound through the foothills and down through the streets of a deserted city. The remains of the entire city were covered with a thick mantel of gray volcanic dust.

To the west she spotted a few rectangular structures rising out of an expansive inland sea, then recognized them as the tops of what must have been high-rise buildings.

She flew to the east to investigate a thin wisp of smoke rising from the edge of a forest, discovered a small band of people living in wooden shelters. *Survivors of some dark and violent natural disaster?*

The disturbing vision startled her awake. She struggled to recapture the deep intuitive understanding that had briefly passed through her, but it was gone.

* * * * *

The too familiar, bone-chilling nightmare visited her again in the cool, still dawn.

The beast was upon her.

Diana threw herself from the bed. Instantly she had sword in hand and was squarely on her feet in the warrior's stance. She wrapped all her senses together – saw, felt, listened, smelled, and became every part of the hut. Nothing seemed to be there, and yet...

She moved cautiously to the doorway and peered out through the net onto the porch. There was no evidence of the fearsome beast that had fallen upon her.

Only at Chat Chew's curious "Mee...ow" from the

bed did she realize that the terrifying vision must had truly appeared in a nightmare.

"That was no dream," she whispered. "It was far too real for a dream." She slowly turned in a full circle, but again found nothing unusual.

Diana sat cross-legged on the bed until the sky began to lighten.

The terrible vision of the dragon did not return.

* * * * *

The Morning Parrot's shriek ended her vigil. Diana walked to the door for her morning run, then instead went back for her sword and set out on the path to Marieji's hut.

"Marieji," she called out from the path outside the hut. "Are you here?" She had learned to expect an attack at any moment, and from any direction. Since returning from her vision quest she had been stalked day and night. Her senses had been refined and polished to a fine edge.

A warm breeze brushed lightly against her back.

Diana dropped her weight and threw her hands out at chest level to fend off an attack. No one was there, yet she still had the sense of something stalking her. She sniffed at the breeze, listened for the source of the threat.

The breeze shifted slightly. Diana slapped her right hand onto the handle of her sword. "Marieji," she shouted, "I feel you tracking me. You won't catch me unaware."

A parrot sprang into the air from the large Palma tree directly behind her. Diana spun around, sword drawn and ready, just as Marieji stepped from behind the tree to challenge her.

"Ah." Marieji threw down a long stick. "I stand down."

Diana stared at her silently, her sword still drawn.

"Is something bothering you? Come on," Marieji motioned. "Let's have a bit of food and talk."

Diana stared vacantly at the piece of fruit in her hand, then looked up to meet Marieji's eyes. "Marieji, last night I had two very disturbing dreams. I flew with the hawk, and ended up above the same blue-green planet I saw on the mountaintop. But this time I really saw it clearly. It looked as though it had been totally torn apart, probably by volcanoes and earthquakes. The cities were under water. I only saw little villages of people. Do you think it was—"

"Do I think it was your Earth?" Marieji interrupted. "Is that your question?"

Diana nodded.

"We've talked about this before, Diana. As you now realize, the Earth herself is a multi-dimensional conscious being. And like all such beings, she has a natural tendency to evolve. Some believe the Earth has her own goal of growing into ever higher states of being, just as we do."

"You're saying the Earth has consciousness, Marieji?"

"The nature of life itself is consciousness, so how could the Earth not also have consciousness?"

"But, higher states?"

"Look at it this way, Diana. Maybe what some call higher states are just faster levels of vibration. And what they call different dimensions are just different positions on one continuous scale of vibratory frequencies."

"Like you said before – different notes on a musical scale. But are you saying that Earth could exist at two different levels of vibration at the same time?"

"Of course. She already does. The ancient alchemists were right when they said 'As it is above, so it is below.' Is there only one note on a scale? Hardly. Many exist simultaneously."

"I get it."

"Like all of us, the Earth vibrates in a certain dominant frequency. So of course the beings on the Earth have their physical senses naturally keyed into seeing and hearing within that frequency. But Earth's base frequency has changed…and will change yet again during the Great Change. It has already started to do so."

"Is that what my vision is all about. Will all those earthquakes and volcanoes cause Earth's frequency to change?"

"No. The Earth is coming to the end of a long season, the Tibetans call it a *yuga*, and is preparing to focus her consciousness at a faster vibration – a higher frequency. The earthquakes, volcanoes and violent weather patterns aren't the cause. They're just the outward manifestation of an internal transformational process. Growth and change aren't always necessarily gentle, as you know."

"But what will happen to mankind? I saw a great city under water."

"Those who manage to adapt to and hold Earth's evolving higher frequency will naturally manifest in that new frequency – be part of it. But those who hold fast to the old will basically see only death and destruction...and will likely be consumed by their own fear and despair."

"There's already a lot of fear and despair on Earth."

"Indeed. But those who manage to transform themselves along with the Earth, to adapt to her new level of vibration, will do more than survive. They'll find themselves living in quite an exciting, dynamic place."

Marieji gazed off into the jungle.

She's a gold mine of information, Diana thought. It had seemed to her for years that time was moving faster. *Was that a result of a faster vibratory level? Had there already been a change in the basic vibrational frequency of the Earth? If so, would it be detectable? Or would it be somehow invisible, since everything else on Earth would automatically be relative to that basic vibration? And what would happen to mankind? Is there any hope?*

"Calm your mind, Diana." Marieji touched her arm and handed her a piece of cut melon. "Incredible things can happen when a person's security is snatched from them. Courage and resourcefulness can spring forth like a newly planted garden, simply because there's nothing to lose. Have faith. Worry just limits your ability to accept transformation."

Diana breathed deeply and gazed out into the jungle. "Marieji," she said softly, "I also saw the dragon in my dreams last night. But it wasn't like a dream. It seemed very real." She shivered as a brief glimpse of her dream crept through the back of her mind.

"You clearly saw the dragon?"

"Yes, I felt its breath on me in the darkness."

Marieji stood and lifted her sheathed sword from a peg just inside the door, motioned for Diana to follow her. "Come. The time is upon you, Diana."

"What time?"

"You must prepare to face the dragon."

"But Marieji, I'm not ready."

"Listen to me carefully, Diana," Marieji said slowly. "If you wait until you feel ready, you'll never face any of your fears – let alone the dragon. Go to the waterfall and stand ready. I'm coming to test you, and you may not recognize my form."

* * * * *

Diana stepped onto the path to the waterfall and set out in a measured lope. The feeling of being tracked by some sinister force still hung over her.

She slowed to a cautious walk as she neared the waterfall. Satisfied that Marieji hadn't yet arrived, she dropped to one knee, cupped water into her hand for a drink, then rose and stood quietly with her arms to her sides.

She breathed lightly, allowing her body to sway slightly with the cool breeze coming off the river.

A chill suddenly dropped over her.

She held her breath and directed her senses outward. Something very large was in the jungle directly behind her.

She listened, and picked out the deep breathing of an extremely large animal.

The hair rose up on the back of her neck as she also recognized the scent of fresh blood on fur. Something very real was wounded, angry, and poised to attack her.

Run? Turn and fight?

She heard grass and twigs crush as the creature dug its claws into the ground to prepare to leap.

Diana ripped her sword from its sheath and dropped her weight onto the balls of her feet. She spun around to face the sound and leapt backwards into the river, merging with the deep current as it swirled around a huge rock. She let the force of the water carry her downstream.

Seconds later she burst through the surface of the water ten feet downstream – sword-in-hand, and fully alert.

The wounded creature was nowhere to be seen.

"Diana?" Marieji's voice traveled to her from about twenty feet back along the very path she herself had traveled.

"Wait," Diana shouted. "There's danger."

"Watch your fear." Marieji's voice boomed from across the river. "It may be the very thing that is tracking you."

"Marieji?" Diana called softly, still standing in the water. She heard the answer as though it rippled outward from inside her own mind.

I'm here. State your intent.

The sudden thrashing of huge wings cut through the air just behind her. Diana fell to her knees in the waist-deep water – the hilt of her sword instinctively gripped tight against her chest with both hands, the blade rising in front of her face and above her head.

She gasped at the snap of the huge wings breaking out of a dive just behind her head. The shadow of a bird half the size of a hut appeared on the water in front of her.

State your intent, echoed the voice again.

She realized with a deep chill that she was being tested by something far more powerful than herself. Sucking in a deep breath, she rose up from the water and raised her sword above her head.

"I intend to survive," Diana roared at the top of her voice.

"If you intend to survive," the voice thundered back at her from a hundred different directions, "then you must become your intent."

Three howling water spouts taller than the trees suddenly exploded from the river, hung momentarily suspended in mid air, then tore over the surface of the water directly at her.

Diana jammed her sword into its scabbard, leapt from the river, and threw her arms and legs around a tree trunk.

"I am yet alive," she roared as the water spouts collapsed around her feet into an angry pool of muddy water.

"Your intent must burn within you," Marieji's voice thundered at her, shaking the side of the cliff. "You must burn through your fear and become your intent."

Diana leapt to safety from the rocks that began to break loose from the opposite cliff and fly through the air directly at her. She sensed something moving deep inside her gut that felt like a wild animal fully ready to fight to the death.

"I am my intent," she roared back.

Marieji suddenly stepped to the edge of the river on the

opposite shore, palms up to show that she held no weapon. "That's enough," she said. "Come with me."

* * * * *

Marieji stood to poke the fire, then settled back onto a fallen tree trunk across from Diana. "We have one more thing to consider," she said.

Diana now knew that tone of voice well. It called for total focus and careful listening. She straightened her back, nodded readiness.

Marieji hesitated and gazed at Diana through the wavering heat of the fire. "Diana, you have demonstrated you can stand present in the moment. You have also shown courage and skill in the warrior's arts. I feel you can select a goal and achieve it in the face of great odds. All of this is very good…but one thing is still missing."

"What's that?"

"You haven't yet faced the truth of your being."

"The truth of my being?" Diana felt the sharp edge of anger cut through her. "Then what's all of this about?"

"You haven't shown a complete understanding of how your attitudes and expectations create all that happens to you."

"Meaning?"

"You are still an innocent – not fully a warrior. Your fear still owns you."

"My fear doesn't own me, Marieji." Diana snapped.

"Is that true?" Marieji asked, shoving her hands into her pockets. "Shall we test that statement?"

"I'm ready."

"You know that you feed energy to anything you give your attention to, don't you? Remember the panther at the cliff?"

"Of course I do."

"Then you also realize that when you're afraid, you feed energy to the very thing you fear."

Diana shrugged, waited.

Marieji suddenly jumped to her feet, shrieked a mind-splitting cry, and threw a handful of dust into the fire.

A firestorm exploded from the fire.

Diana's cried out as the outline of a familiar shape appeared, then formed more solidly. The bright red eyes of the dragon gleamed at her from out of the flames.

"Oh no," Diana gasped. She threw herself backward off the log, rolled desperately into the underbrush, then reached for her sword. She had left it by the log.

Diana ripped her knife from its sheath.

It was too late.

The creature closed down over her, smothering her in a vile cloud of smoke. A burst of orange-yellow fire leapt from the dragon's mouth and exploded in her face. The smell of burning hair filled her nostrils.

"Marieji," she screamed. "Help me."

Then in a flicker of colored lights, the flaming dragon was gone.

"Beware," Marieji called from the darkness. "The stronger your fear, the more certain you will manifest it."

Diana fell to her knees, jammed the blade of her knife into a tree trunk, and heaved up burning acid and bile.

* * * * *

She walked back to the village alone in the darkness – her dread of the dragon, and fear of her own probable death, tracking her every step.

CⱭ⅏

CHAPTER TWENTY THREE

The only way to discover the limits of the possible
is to go beyond them...into the impossible.

—*Arthur C. Clark*

THE MORNING PARROT had just burst forth with song when
Diana sensed, rather than heard, someone step onto the porch
of her hut.

Danger? Her hand flashed to the hilt of her sword just
beneath the bed.

"No need for your sword, my warrior," Marieji called
out from the porch. "Something tells me you just need to
share your thoughts with a friend this morning."

My nerves are a wreck, Diana thought. *How does she
keep sneaking up on me like that? It's driving me raving mad.*
She traced the scar on her knee with a fingertip. She felt deeply
tired. Discouraged. Beaten. What good had all of this done?
She had collapsed in the face of an imaginary dragon.

She dressed and went out onto the porch.

Marieji nodded to her silently.

Diana settled onto the porch a respectful distance from the older woman. She pulled Chat Chew onto her lap for moral support, then ran her fingers lightly over the spot where the flames had burned the hair off her right arm.

"What did you dream of last night?"

Diana shuddered. "The dragon. It came again. And I'm certain I visited myself in the hospital again, Marieji. I feel death tracking me – my own death."

"Diana, for the past week you have seen both the dragon and the hospital every night in your dreams. The time has come to stand in the face of your fear. You must go today to the dragon's peak."

The full length of Diana's spine snapped. "Today? Oh my God, Marieji. I can't."

"You must."

"But, last night you…you tested me, and I totally failed."

Marieji sniffed lightly at the breeze. "True. You do still carry a very distinct scent of fear about you."

"What's wrong with me?" Diana sighed. "I feel as though no matter how hard I try, I still face certain defeat."

"It's far better to focus on what's right with you, then move forward from there."

"But Marieji, why did I do that last night?"

"Because on a deep level, your fear still owns you. You must remember Diana – if you allow yourself to fear defeat, you'll create defeat by feeding it energy."

Until the incident by the fire, she had felt as though she

was doing well. But now she felt totally exhausted – felt it throughout her entire being. *There has to be some way out of this*, she told herself. *Marieji wouldn't really just send me off to my death, would she?*

"Diana, you know that what you focus on is certain to grow, until it finally owns you."

"Marieji," she sighed. "How can I ever overcome my fear? It feels like its just part of me. Always has been."

Silence.

"Diana, you chose the ultimate warrior's adventure – be challenged by deep trauma, then use the stimulus of that trauma to restore yourself to being fully alive."

"Marieji. What if I instead choose to stay on Gaia? Maybe–"

Marieji shook her head.

"Marieji–"

"Diana, stop feeding your fear."

"But last night at the fire – the dragon. If I could stop being afraid I would. It's not something I can just turn on and off. I'm not ready to face the dragon."

Marieji sighed and lifted one finger for silence. "All right Diana. Let's take a look at the part of yourself you left in that Earth hospital. Then perhaps you'll understand why you have to go." She patted the porch boards. "Lie down and close your eyes."

* * * * *

Diana heard two male voices, but discovered she couldn't

open her eyes or move her body.

"All right. Let's get her ready," one of the men said.

"Guess we have no alternative," the other replied.

"Alternative? Are you nuts?" the first man snapped. "I've waited too long already for a cranial exploratory. She's set up for Op Two. The orderlies will bring her down. Let's go scrub."

Diana heard the shuffling of feet around her – felt two sets of strong arms slide under her, lift her, then place her down on a hard surface and cover her with a cold sheet.

An unpleasant dizziness swept over her as she heard the sound of wheels, then realized she was being moved somewhere on a rolling table. She tried to move her arms, but they flailed out of control.

"Crap," she heard one of the men snap. "You better hold her arms down until we can get restraints back on her. Gezz. Grab her! They'll bust our butts if she pops that IV loose."

"Hey," the other man answered, "get off my case. I can't help it if she's having a seizure or something."

"Get that IV. Cripes."

"Stop this gurney and I'll move the strap down over her forearms."

"We should've put wrist restraints on her."

"Yeah?" he growled, "well neither of those two docs told us to."

The motion stopped. Diana listened to the footsteps echo down a long hallway.

Where am I?

A crackle burst from a speaker on the wall above her. "Dr. Longer to ER. Dr. Longer to ER."

Oh no. I'm definitely in a hospital. But...but why can't I see? She tried unsuccessfully to open her eyes, then heard a door swing open.

"Got her Mary," an official-sounding female voice announced.

Again the uncomfortable sensation of floating as the gurney was pushed across the floor.

The bright lights of the operating theater assaulted Diana's closed eyelids, creating an image of a bright red sun and swirling, green-yellow clouds. She watched the clouds pulsate across the insides of her eyelids with the fascination of a child.

Then she heard a scraping sound as someone adjusted an ultra-bright lamp so that the light fell directly onto her face. The pattern of lights on her inner eyelids was no longer pleasant.

Diana was shocked to feel her lips move as if on their own. "Too bright," she heard herself mumble thickly.

Sudden silence.

"Do you think she's trying to talk?" One of the female voices gasped.

"Are you kidding?" a male voice barked. "Just a response to those bright lights."

"Think we should sedate and proceed with pre-op?" The female voice asked.

"No operation," Diana heard herself mumble. "No..."

"Of course we proceed," the man with the raspy voice snapped. "We've got the room scheduled and she's ready to go.

Let's not forget, I'm the senior intern here."

"No operation," Diana heard herself rasp thickly, then realized she could now see the entire scene, although her eyes were still glued shut.

Diana watched a nurse move to the head of the table and begin to set up a chrome-plated head restraint near her shaved head. Another nurse draped her body from the chin down with a sheet, then filled a hypodermic from a clear vile. She covered the end of the needle with a swab of alcohol-soaked cotton and placed it on a metal prep tray.

"Let's go," the dark-haired intern with the raspy voice snapped.

The blond intern standing beside him held up his hand. "I don't know Marc," he said. "I think we'd better hold off until Dr. Brennan joins us."

"What in blazes for, Bob?" The dark-haired intern snarled.

The blond intern folded his arms in front of his chest. "Marc, I think she might be coming out of the coma."

"Because she mumbled some nonsense sounds? Are you totally nuts? She's mine. I've waited six months for a cranial exploratory." The dark-haired intern straightened his back and braced his shoulders. "I say we pre-sedate and get ready for Brennan."

The blond intern pushed the nurse back, then bent over Diana. "Do you know where you are?" he asked.

"Hos..." She mumbled. "Hos...pi ..."

"Did you hear that, Marc," the blond intern said. "She's giving clear evidence of consciousness."

The dark-haired intern sneered, snatched the hypodermic from the prep tray, and jabbed the needle into Diana's arm.

"Stop. Marc." The blond intern yelled.

"No operrr...aaa...." Diana rasped more loudly. Her eyes rolled behind her closed eyelids.

The blond intern bent over Diana, then stood up and glared at the other intern. "Marc, I'm reporting this to Brennan. You better stop this whole procedure." He peeled off his gloves, threw them to the floor, spun on his heel and jolted toward the door of the operating room.

"Anyone else having a problem?" The dark-haired intern rasped at the two nurses. "You both know that my uncle heads the administration of this institution, don't you?"

The two masked nurses looked silently at each other over Diana's immobile body, then dropped their eyes.

The three of them turned as the senior surgeon they knew as "the Bear" backed into the operating theater holding his scrubbed hands out in front of him. He jammed his hands into the gloves held out for him by the younger nurse.

"Where's Bob?" He growled.

"I think he lost it Dr. Brennan," the dark-haired intern shrugged. "He ran out the door insisting that the patient was coming out of her coma."

"What made him think that?" Brennan barked.

"She was mumbling some nonsense sounds."

"Hasn't she done that on and off since she was admitted?" the older doctor asked.

"I don't think so, Dr. Brennan," one of the nurses answered in a low voice. "At least not that I know of."

"Any other unusual behavior?" Brennan barked.

"Eyes rolled around strangely for a while," the other nurse replied in a flat voice.

"Is that it?" Brennan snapped. "What did Bob think he was doing leaving the operating theater like that? I'll bust his– Oh crap. Let's go, Marc. Screw her down."

"But…Dr. Marc already injected her," the older nurse stammered.

"He did what?"

"Yes sir. Almost twenty minutes ago."

"What's going on here, Marc. She's not even set up. What did you think you were doing?"

Have to stay awake, Diana thought. She watched her own arms begin to flail.

The older doctor grabbed her arms. "Why isn't she restrained," he snapped. "I thought this was the comatose Jane Doe."

"It is, sir."

Diana moaned and mumbled a nonsense sound.

"Girl," Brennan growled at the younger nurse. "Hook her up to that EEG monitor. I want to see that brainwave activity Dr. White has been carrying on about."

"But she's already had pre-op injection sir," the intern protested. "Don't you think we should just–"

"Just hook her up. Now."

The older nurse grabbed a squeeze bottle and cotton and quickly swabbed just behind each of Diana ears. She peeled the backs off two pre-glued sensor pads and pressed them into place, attached long leads from the EEG monitor, and keyed a command into the keyboard.

A complex pattern of colored lines appeared on the monitor suspended a few feet behind the operating table.

"Give me a typical from her historic recordings," Brennan barked.

The nurse keyed in a command.

The screen divided in the middle – the top part frozen, the bottom showing Diana's current brain activity.

The entire team turned around as the blond intern burst through the scrub room door. "Dr. Brennan," he shouted. "I came looking for you. She came out of her coma. We can't just–"

"Bob…" The dark-haired intern communicated an implied warning to the other intern.

"We have a schedule on this room, Doctor," Brennan yelled. "What did you think you were doing leaving the operating theater like that?"

"Doctor Brennan." The blond intern jammed his hands into the gloves held out for him by the nurse. "The patient spoke. She knows she's in an operating room."

No operation. No operation. Diana silently repeated in her mind as she struggled against the effects of the injection.

Brennan looked back up at the monitor. So what are all those alpha and beta spikes about?" Brennan jabbed his chin at the monitor. "What's going on here?"

"Probably just a reaction to the lights and stimulation," the dark-haired intern hissed.

"Dr. Brennan," the blond intern pleaded. "She was

conscious and coherent. She–"

"She what?" Brennan shouted at the agitated intern.

"I asked her if she knew where she was. It sounded like she said 'hospital'."

"Sounded like? Is that right, Marc?" Brennan spun to face the dark-haired intern.

"I heard nonsense mumbling," he shrugged.

Got to stay awake, Diana thought desperately. *Got to…*

"So…" Brennan focused again on the brainwave readings. "What do you doctors say about those brainwaves?"

"Just random beta and alpha in response to the operating room stimulation," the dark-haired intern insisted. "She's my teaching case, sir. In my opinion we should proceed with the planned exploratory brain surgery."

"This is a very high risk procedure, Marc – with a very low probability of meaningful mental survival."

The dark-haired intern shrugged his shoulders. "I still say those alpha and beta spikes are just non-coherent activity."

"OK," Brennan shrugged. "Let's proceed."

No, Diana screamed in her mind. *Don't cut open my brain.*

The tracings on the brainwave screen went wild.

Brennan held up his hand. "Look at that. Odd. Not necessarily coherent, but–" He looked at the clock and shook his head. "We've already wasted too much time on all this. Get her out of here and reschedule for tomorrow – early."

C8∂

CHAPTER TWENTY FOUR

It does not matter what our specific fate is,
so long as we face it with ultimate abandon.

—*Carlos Castaneda/Don Juan*

DIANA OPENED HER eyes and was relieved to see Marieji sitting next to her on the porch. "Marieji, I–"

"I know Diana. I traveled with you to be sure you could return safely."

Diana gulped back the lump in her throat, opened her mouth to speak, and had to force the words out. "I guess what you've told me is true. I already face possible death, or worse."

"That's true, Diana."

Diana pulled in a long, ragged breath. "Either at the hands of those surgeon, or when I face the dragon. What's the use?"

"Look around you at nature," Marieji continued. "Life is a process of constant transformation. Death is simply an intimate part of that ongoing transformation."

Diana sighed deeply.

Marieji hesitated and gazed deeply into Diana's eyes. "You do realize that consciousness survives death, don't you?"

"Marieji, I…I haven't personally seen any evidence of life after death."

"Diana, you already know that the essence of what you call 'yourself' isn't solid at all. And even if you could manage to get hold of all the so-called solid matter on Earth at the same time and pack it together, it would all fit inside your fist. Everything is made up of energy in motion. Your body, your mind are no exception."

"So?"

"Suppose you put some metal filings on a piece of paper and hold them in place with a magnet on the other side of the paper. When you take the magnet away, the metal filings will scatter, true. But do they de-manifest?"

"Of course not."

"Diana, one of the most important things you must come to understand is what it means to die. Your true self is like the magnet. It's what existed before you were born. It had to precede you, or what would have collected all those atoms together to create your body and mind in the first place? What you call death is nothing more than a refocus of that magnet – the core of your true self – at a higher energy level."

"So you're claiming that physical death won't be the end of my life?"

"No. I'm saying you could have an alternative. Many on Earth today are in early stages of dream-learning to consciously transfer their focus from one dimension to another by changing the vibratory level of their physical being. They will welcome the energy of the Great Change – use it to rearrange their molecular structure to take quantum leaps into other planes of existence. Many feel that more advanced beings are already reaching to the earth plane to support this effort."

"Gads, Marieji. As a child I used to dream of walking through walls. Was that–"

"Yes, walking through walls is much the same concept. Your higher self was clearly sending you a message. It was reminding you of one of your primary life goals."

"So…what is death then?"

"Diana, you studied science in school. Do you remember the basic law that energy can be neither created nor destroyed? The energy essence of yourself is already, and has always been, immortal. Think about it. If the life force didn't survive physical death, life would simply have perished following the death of the first simple life forms."

"Huh," Diana shook her head. *I hadn't thought of that. It's so straightforward, and obviously true.*

"Many persons on Earth are having lucid near-death experiences that clearly point to the truth of this – beautiful experiences that have allowed them to glimpse beyond the veil separating the everyday world from a far richer place of being. This is no make-believe heaven. What they've seen is a glimpse of the heart of the life force. We're each made up of the essence of that force. How could we be made up of anything else? What you call physical death is simply a return to our true nature – to our true source."

Diana watched a monkey drop from a tree and race along

the path. "OK," she sighed. "OK Marieji. I'll face the dragon. But I can't claim to be anything other afraid. No matter what you say, I really don't want to die."

Marieji nodded, picked up the carrying bag lying next to her and handed it to Diana. "This is for your journey."

She took the bag and inspected the finely detailed hand-painted scenes of a woman fighting a dragon. Even the leather strap was painted with intricate detail. She opened an outside pocket and pulled out a new canteen with a leather thong. From another side pocket she extracted a bag of dried fruit and some algae bars. Beneath was a larger bag of oats.

"For TwoSox," Marieji smiled.

Diana pulled out a straw hat fitted with a rolled leather chin cord. Just beneath the hat was a roll of sterile white cloth, a jar of the salve that Olji had put on her head wound, and a snake bite kit.

She lifted out a large net bag, opened it to examine a coil of rope and one of the tightly woven water resistant sheets that served the villagers as both a rain poncho, and the roof of a temporary shelter while traveling. Near the bottom she found a small cooking pot packed with dried vegetables and bits of jerky. On the very bottom was a spare pair of gum-soled shoes.

Diana repacked the carrying-bag in silence. She looked down at Chat Chew, now sitting next to her on the porch, then out at the jungle. This place had taken her heart. She truly felt she belonged on Gaia. A heavy sadness fell over her.

"Diana, like the Earth, you too may be preparing to leap into new vibratory levels. If you return successfully, you must be certain to visit some of Earth's ancient power places. This will greatly accelerate your development."

"Marieji, even if I do manage to return, how will I ever apply what I've learned here to my life on Earth? It's not like I can stroll around LA wearing a sword. It seems as though all of this effort will be just...just wasted if I go back."

Marieji nodded appreciation of her question. "You may be surprised. Remember that every experience you have, every thought you think, changes you forever. Even what you call dreams and visions are impressed on your deepest mind. All of this will remain part of your being – your true self."

"You mean I'll remember all of this?"

"If you manage to return before the surgeons slice into your brain, yes. You probably won't consciously recall your experience at first. But then things will begin to happen that will trigger your memory, although at first it may seem like *deja vu's*. And I expect you will be drawn to like-minded people, and to a teacher who can help you continue to develop. Your deepest inner self won't forget what you've learned. It can't forget."

"A teacher?"

"When you're truly hungry for knowledge Diana, life itself becomes your teacher. But to answer your question, a teacher already awaits you. Assuming you're able to successfully pass through the gate, that is."

"But if I succeed, how will I find this teacher?"

"You'll be drawn to her. Remember – there are no accidents, Diana. And if you open yourself to her wisdom, she'll guide you into even deeper realms of being and a readiness to actively participate in the Great Change –

to rise up with the Phoenix."

"Participate?"

"Diana. As the ancient prophecies come alive and the Great Change moves closer, people will look desperately for new ways to deal with the chaos and destruction around them. You may be called upon to share your understanding of how we create our reality with our thoughts and intentions."

"You mean…the oceans rising…that desert-like wilderness is really happening?"

"I've told you – that's one probable reality."

"Depressing, Marieji." Diana rubbed the back of her neck. " I really can't bear to believe you."

"Diana, on Gaia we understand these changes are necessary for the Earth. It's just part of her transformation. Don't worry, if you manage to successfully pass through the gate you can rebuild yourself as a warrior and ride the Great Change joyfully."

Diana's mind swelled with visions tumbling one over the other – of a great desert spreading over the land…a thin ribbon of smoke rising from a little settlement on a mountainside…a huge inland sea…

"Diana. Say good by to your friend there," Marieji nodded at Chat Chew, "then dress in your riding gear and prepare TwoSox. Corsa is waiting for you. She'll ride with you to the edge of the jungle."

Diana stared off into the jungle.

Marieji stood up with a definite finality. "Just remember this," she extended a hand to help Diana to her feet. "Stay focused in the now. The only true point of power is in the present moment." Marieji held Diana by her shoulders, her dark eyes gleaming with intensity. "But above all else, Diana, beware that you don't thrust the sword into your own heart, just to escape your fear."

Marieji's words burned into her mind.

* * * * *

Diana pulled TwoSox up beside Corsa's large mare, swung her right leg over the saddle and slid lightly to the ground. She automatically looped the reins loosely in her hand, then led TwoSox into the small a respectful distance from the other horse.

"Keep your eyes on her," Corsa called out as Diana moved downstream. "There are all kinds of surprises here at the edge of the jungle. And be sure to fill your canteens up to the very top."

Diana stood and looked out over the barren wasteland that stretched every direction from the edge of the jungle. Her stomach growled with nervous tension; a sharp headache rose from her shoulders into the back of her head. She shook her head. *If only I didn't have to go.*

Corsa glanced at Diana, then waded across the shallow stream.

They stood side by side and gazed out across the barren badlands toward the imposing western mountains.

"Diana," Corsa said in a low voice. "You realize that to stand before the dragon, you must be willing to face the almost certain death of what you call yourself?"

Diana stared out over the sun-scorched badlands. "Marieji told me," she replied quietly.

"Many have failed. It's far easier to simply surrender to fear, than to face the truth of your own being."

"No doubt."

Corsa pointed to the needle-like point on the mountain range. "See the highest point?"

Diana nodded. She had become very familiar with the peak during her vision quest, and now saw it constantly it her mind's eye. It was the dragon's peak.

"Head directly for it. You'll come to a narrow creek at the bottom of the mountain. Spend the night there. Be sure to keep TwoSox hobbled and tied. You'll feel the dragon."

"Feel it?"

"Oh yes," Corsa said quietly. "It will take all of your courage to climb the cliff and seek the gate. But just let your intent lead you. You can't miss it." Corsa went to the horses and led TwoSox over to Diana. "Now go," she looked up to judge the position of the sun. "Ride straight toward the peak. You'll be there before nightfall."

"Corsa? I just want to–"

Corsa grabbed her shoulders and embraced her roughly. "Just remember, Diana. No matter what happens, stay out of the dark place."

"The dark place?"

"The caves. You'll see them. Now go."

Diana mounted and relaxed the reins to give TwoSox one a long drink from the stream. She positioned the straw hat on her head, then urged the reluctant mare from the stream and out onto the badlands.

"Remember Diana," Corsa called after her. "Your thoughts are your most powerful weapon. They're far more powerful than your sword."

Diana turned and watched Corsa and her mare disappear into the jungle.

* * * * *

She reined in TwoSox and turned in the saddle to look back at the jungle. Intense heat bounced off the dry sand, reducing the jungle to a wavy, faint mirage. She turned back toward the distant mountain range and coaxed TwoSox forward with a slight pressure of her knees. The mare moved out easily, allowing Diana to guide her in the direction of the forbidding needle peak.

She soon found herself surrounded only by faceless rocks, barren bushes, an occasional desert creature, and the relentless sun. The jungle had disappeared completely.

Diana pulled TwoSox up at the creek just as the sun dropped behind the needle-like peak. *Corsa was right*, she thought. *I can definitely feel the dragon. Definitely.*

සිද

CHAPTER TWENTY FIVE

There is no medium between us and the
Universal Mind except our own thoughts.

—Ernest Holmes

DIANA DISMOUNTED AND pulled the saddle off TwoSox, then stood and scanned her surroundings. Her eyes fell on a natural camp site bounded on two sides by thick clusters of slender trees – the cliff to the rear.

TwoSox grazed on the thick grass along the side of the creek while Diana investigated the trees. A quick glance identified what she was looking for. She drew her sword and cut a deep V into the base of a thick limb, snapped it free, then quickly cut two more limbs and dragged all three to the clearing.

She stripped the smaller branches from the limbs, leaving a fork at the end of two of the limbs. With a few swift blows she then sharpened the ends to sharp points, and finally hammered the sharpened ends of the poles into the ground with a flat rock.

She stripped the third limb to form a cross pole and positioned it across the two forked limbs, then grabbed an armful of the smaller limbs, snapped off their leaves, and stacked them against the cross pole to form a rough lean-to framework. Finally she stretched the water resistant sheet over the structure, tied the edges in place, and anchored the bottom edge with a few large rocks.

Diana stood back to admire her handiwork. "Not bad." She snorted at the memory of how totally hopeless her camping skills had been before Sola had taken her in hand. Her first lean-to had collapsed on her during the night.

She snapped the leaves off the remaining branches and arranged them in a neat pile under the shelter to serve as a bed. Finally she positioned the saddle to block the end of the shelter where she would rest her head.

Finally she tossed her bedroll into the shelter, and began to collect large rocks for her fire pit.

* * * * *

By the time the first stars appeared Diana had seen to TwoSox and had a pot of jerky stew positioned on a flat rock surrounded by hot coals.

She shook some dry bread flour into her drinking cup, added some water, and kneaded the mixture into a small handful of dough. She rolled the dough into a long strip, then wound it around the end of a green stick she had peeled and tempered in the fire. She pinched the rolled edges tight and propped her stick bread up over the fire to bake.

"I sure miss Chat Chew," she commented to TwoSox as she moved the mare closer to the campsite for company.

* * * * *

Diana sat for a while after eating, then took her pot and plate downstream and washed them in the moonlight with sand and water.

Too restless to sleep, she lay looking up into the night sky. The air was thick with the scent of Gaia sage and purple Lavendo. She listened to the songs of the great night birds, fought off some mosquito-like insects, and forced herself to think of anything except the dragon.

The fire burned itself down into dusty embers before she finally surrendered to a very uneasy sleep. Her dreams were tormented by on-going visions of herself strapped down totally helpless in a hospital bed.

* * * * *

Diana breathed deeply in the early morning air. *So very different from the jungle,* she noted. *Too dry. And…so still.*

A long note sang out from the gathering of trees by the creek as the first molark awakened. Then what she had taken for a barren wasteland exploded into life just as the first tip of the sun hit the top of the dragon's peak.

She took a moment to salute the sun – a new habit since she had come to Gaia. But the early morning sunlight felt totally unlike that of the lush, green jungle. The intensity of the rays instantly stung and pricked at her skin like a harsh chemical.

A memory of how the California sun had changed in the winter of '92 rushed through her. *Was this zone depletion too?* That was the year she had first really noticed how the sun felt different – far too intense, even in mid-winter.

She looked out over the wasteland. "Is this really where Earth is headed?" she sighed.

The intensity of the sun continued to grow as Diana repacked her carrying bag. She picked up her speed – strode to the creek, filled both canteens, then tied one to her bag and the other to her belt.

She stood for a moment contemplating the cliff she would have to climb, then went to TwoSox. In a few sure movements she had the skittish mare saddled. She then lashed the bridle to the saddle, removed her hobbles, and tied them to the saddle horn.

Diana gently led TwoSox to the stream for a long drink. The mare seemed to know what was ahead of her. She drank long and deep, then lifted her head and shook her mane restlessly.

Diana pressed her cheek against her the horse's velvety neck. "TwoSox," she sighed. "I wish I could ride you back to the jungle. But I can't. I have to say goodbye now."

Heaviness settled into her chest. She gulped back the lump in her throat, removed the rope halter and lead rope, and tied them to the back of the saddle, then quickly slapped the mare solidly on her flank.

"Go home, TwoSox" she shouted.

She cupped a hand above her eyes and watched TwoSox confidently gallop off in the direction of the jungle.

She was now truly alone.

Diana surveyed the cliff that rose high above her, debating on the best approach to scaling it. *I'm about to climb up that cliff,* she thought. *Me. About to climb a sheer cliff.* She shook her head in amazement at how her ideas of what was possible had changed since coming to Gaia.

Diana slung her carrying bag over her shoulders. Her first handhold was a deep crack between two rocks pressed together by tons of rock and dirt.

She stopped for a brief rest on a tiny ledge.

I'm really part of this place now, she thought as she looked down onto the wasteland. *And I like who I've become. How can I ever be like this on Earth? In LA?* Her right foot slipped as part of the ledge gave way.

"Get present," she ordered herself.

She repositioned her feet, took a long drink from her canteen and resumed her climb.

* * * * *

Waves of intense mid-morning heat were bouncing off the dusty red rocks by the time Diana pulled herself up onto the huge plateau. There was no visible shelter from the sun.

She clambered up onto a large rock formation and turned slowly to scan her surroundings. An odd patch of thick fog at the base of the needle peak caught her attention. She defocused her eyes to take in a broader picture. *Impossible,* she thought. *How could there be fog in such a hot, dry place?*

She climbed down off the rocks and set out in a straight line directly toward the unexpected patch of fog.

* * * * *

Diana hesitated at the sharp border of the foggy cloud.

This whole scene is wrong, she thought. *How can there be fog in this heat?*

She rubbed her eyes and tried to look into the thick grayness. It was impenetrable. She sniffed at the air and recognized the faint scent of sulfur.

"Follow your nose," she mumbled

She slipped into the cloud of fog, the clear smell of sulfur drawing her deeper into the thick gray-white blanket. A tingling sensation crawled over her scalp as the scent grew stronger and stronger.

She felt her fear tracking her.

This is hopeless, she thought. *There's no way to possibly see clearly in here.* She squinted her eyes nearly closed to intensify her other senses, then suddenly jolted to a stop. Her warrior's training had stopped her at the very edge of a cliff. She cautiously stepped backward.

A few steps in the opposite direction ended at a small pool of water hidden in the fog. An even thicker mist swirled across its surface and hung thick and foreboding just above the surface of the pool.

"Too small to create all of this fog," she commented. She dipped one finger into the pool and tasted the water. "Not the source of that bad smell, either."

She groped her way around the small pool, then sat down in a small thicket to wait for the fog to lift. *This whole dragon thing is probably just another of Marieji's tricks,* she thought.

Her eyes were drawn to a thumbnail-sized reddish brown spider mending its web in a small clump of reed just a hand's span from her face. Suddenly a blue fly whizzed by her head. One strand of the silvery web caught its wing. The blue fly catapulted around the strand, landing head-first in the web.

Diana watched, darkly fascinated, as the spider moved in on its prey and quickly threw strands silvery cable around the fly. She thought of the dragon, and identified uneasily with the fly.

An odd sensation suddenly jolted her out of her reverie. She came to full alert as a loud whoosh of what could only be huge wings swirled the fog into a vortex around the small pool. The ground trembled as she threw herself flat .

Marieji? She thought out into the fog.

No one answered.

The earth trembled again.

Then through the swirling fog she saw a large, dark form moving about.

Marieji? She thought again with all of her intent, reaching out through the fog for any sign of her mentor.

No answer came.

Diana lifted her head and peered out from behind the thicket.

The top of what looked like a spiny ridge of pointed fins was visible just above the top layer of fog.

Her mind froze.

Huge wings opened, stretched and flapped. Clouds of fog swirled up into the air and immediately burned off in the intense heat.

No way, she protested. *It has to be Marieji playing with my mind again.*

As the fog disappeared, Diana rose to her knees and stared in total amazement at the huge creature. "Oh my God," she gasped. "It's a…a real dragon." Intense red lights flashed on and off inside her head.

Marieji? She reached out desperately, hopefully, with her thoughts.

The dragon snorted.

Diana wrinkled her nose as a sulfurous cloud assaulted her nostrils and eyes. Panic twisted at her stomach.

The dragon stood up on its massive hind legs and snorted again, then rotated its head to look from one end of the plateau to the other.

A gleaming red eye suddenly pinned her. The beast settled back onto all four feet and looked directly at her.

Diana leapt to her feet, eyes peeled open in shock. Her face burst into flames as the blood rushed to her head.

She ripped her sword from its sheath and stood frozen. Her dreams had not deceived her. The dragon was as big as a house. She recalled the fate of the blue fly.

The huge creature stared at her – a blinding light bursting from its huge crystalline eyes. Huge scarlet nostrils flared broadly with each breath.

Diana stood transfixed as the remaining fog lifted from around the dragon and the sun began to gather on its multi-colored body. Each of its shining rainbow scales glistened in the sunlight like highly polished mirrors. She found herself staring into endless mirror-like images of herself standing sword-in-hand before the dragon.

The plateau was silent except for the great creature's steady, deep breathing.

The dragon suddenly lifted its wings.

Diana gasped as it lowered its great head almost to the ground, eyes blazing. Its chest expanded as it sucked in a deep breath.

She suddenly realized from her dreams – the dragon was about to hurl a fireball at her. She dropped her sword, spun around, scrambled to the edge of the cliff and desperately grabbed the base of a spiny burr bush.

She ignored the painful slash of burr bush spines cutting into her hand and she catapulted over the side of the cliff just as the fireball rocketed over her head.

She scrabbled for a foothold, gave up, dropped onto a small ledge, then looked up to two red eyes peering over the edge just two arm-lengths above her.

Without stopping to think, Diana grabbed a scrub brush growing out of the side of the cliff, threw herself off the ledge sideways, and dropped to an outcropping of sharp rocks a few feet below.

A fireball shattered the foothold she had just stood on.

The dragon's roar sent a cascade of rocks crashing down over her head. She threw her body against the side of the cliff, then spotted a faint animal trail about ten feet beneath her. She desperately grabbed a scrappy clump of grass for a handhold, kicked her feet free as it came off in her hand, and slid on her belly down the face of the cliff.

The moment her feet hit the narrow trail, Diana sprinted toward what looked like a large cave about a hundred feet down the trail.

She threw herself into the cave and collapsed to her knees. From out of the darkness she watched the dragon snort at her discarded carrying bag, then walk back toward the pool. Her sword, gleaming in the sun where she had dropped it, seemed of no interest to the great beast.

Diana collapsed onto the floor of the cave. Her body twisted into a tight ball, overcome with fear and despair, and a torturous wail tore from her throat.

≋

CHAPTER TWENTY SIX

The universe is an infinite agglomeration
of energy fields, resembling threads of light.

—Carlos Castenada/Don Juan

LOST IN THE depths of her pain, Diana was totally unaware of
the eyes that watched her from out of the darkness of the cave.

"Warrior?"

She leapt to her feet and spun around to face the
unexpected voice.

A tall man stepped out of the darkness, holding out open
palms to show that he held no weapon. "I won't hurt you," he
said. "I saw you escape from the dragon."

"You what," she stammered. "How…how did you get
here?"

"I live here," he replied. "We all do."

Several people stepped out of the shadows.

Diana stared at them, speechless.

"That was truly an amazing escape," he said admiringly.

This can't be, Diana protested to herself. *How can this be happening?* Fear twisted at her stomach. She tried to calm her breathing, but a coughing spasm seized her throat. A steady stream of blood dripped from her hand and pooled on the floor of the cave.

What had Corsa told her? "Do not enter the dark place." Was this the cave she had meant?

The sharp pain in her left hand pulled at her attention. Diana looked blankly at the blood dripping from her hand, then back up at the faces surrounding her. *This can't be what Corsa was referring to,* she reassured herself. *These people don't look dangerous.*

"A very exciting escape," a woman's voice added from out of the darkness. The small group moved in closer.

"We must hear your story in council," an older woman added.

Diana looked from one excited face to another. The group moved in closer yet. She cringed as several hands reached out curiously to touch her, then jerked involuntarily as a young boy touched the handle of her knife.

A blond woman stepped forward and held out a handkerchief. "Take this," she said. "Your hand is bleeding."

Diana silently accepted the handkerchief, then stared blankly at the neatly folded piece of cloth.

"Go ahead," the woman said, "wrap it around your hand."

She unfolded the handkerchief and wrapped it around the deep slash in the palm of her left hand.

I should put some salve on it, she thought – then

remembered that she'd left her carrying bag out on the plateau by the dragon.

"I'm the one who saw her first," the tall man said. "I have the right to introduce her."

Diana was amazed as the small group reluctantly turned away at his words and disappeared back into the darkness.

"Who are you?" Diana demanded, her right hand positioned on the handle of her knife.

"A friend," he smiled. "Don't be afraid."

"But, what are all of you doing in this cave?"

"We live here. This is our home."

"Home? Why would you live in this dark cave. The jungle is only a half a day's journey–" Diana swayed, then locked her knees to stabilize herself.

"This is our home," he repeated. "We have no desire to live in the jungle."

"Whew," Diana shrugged. "But so close to the dragon, aren't you afraid that–"

"We are here out of respect for the dragon," he interrupted. "Many of us first came here as you did, to challenge it."

"And?" She gulped back the vile acid pushing up from her stomach into her throat. Her brain was on fire.

"We choose the caves over certain death."

Diana fell silent. It hurt to breath. She shook her head in disbelief. *The dragon is real. It tried to kill me.*

"Since I saw you first," the tall man said, "I have the right to introduce you at council. We'll have a feast in your honor tonight to welcome you."

Her hand was throbbing. Diana swayed.

The stranger thrust an arm around her shoulders to support her. "Let's get that cut taken care of."

Her knees buckled as the burr bush poison started to flow into her blood stream.

* * * * *

Diana was vaguely aware of a familiar smell coming from the scented cloth that had been placed over her mouth and nose. *Ether?* She slipped into a drugged sleep, indifferent to the woman who began to extract pieces of burr bush thorns from the palm of her hand.

She woke groggy. Her left hand throbbed with a dull pain all the way up to her elbow. Someone touched her shoulder, and a brief vision of Marieji flashed through her mind.

"Warrior?"

It was the tall man who had found her.

Diana held up her bandaged hand. "Thank you," she croaked through a dry throat.

"It's a good thing you came here. You had poison burr bush spines in your hand. You could have lost your whole arm. Feel better?"

"Think I need to rest."

"Better to get up and walk off the effects of the herbs. Otherwise they'll stay in your system and you'll feel terrible for days."

Diana let him help her to a seated position.

They had walked only a short distance when the effects of

the herbal anesthesia wore off. A deep, hot pain sliced through her hand and throbbed up into her elbow.

"Want to rest?" He pointed to a rock bench just outside a large storage vault constructed of rocks and dried mud.

Diana collapsed down onto the bench and stared up at the crystalline stalactites hanging down from the roof of the huge cavern. An army of stalagmites reached upward from the floor of the cave to meet them. A single shaft of sunlight had found its way through a small fissure in the ceiling – turning a portion of the ancient salt deposits into a sparkling wall of crystals.

The scene reminded her of something from Earth. A childhood memory played around her mind. *Oh yes,* she recalled. *Carlsbad Caverns.* Millions of years of mineral-rich water dripping from the ceiling of the caves near Carlsbad had created a duplicate environment.

"How do you feel?" he asked.

"OK."

"I wanted to take you to the upper plateau," he sighed. "Perhaps tomorrow morning. We have to get you ready for the council dinner." He stood up. "Come on. I'll show you to the baths."

She followed along with him in uncertain silence.

* * * * *

Fresh clothes and a towel had already been laid out for her. Diana thankfully eased her body into the hot water. *This can't be the "dark place" Corsa spoke of,* she reassured herself. *I can't imagine why anyone would be afraid of this place.*

She dried herself off slowly. *I ran from the dragon. Now what?* She took a long, deep breath to calm her mind. *Later,* she thought. *Not now. So tired.* She slipped on the flowing robe that had been laid out for her.

* * * * *

The sound of laughter and animated conversation drifted down the long hallway as they approached the dining cavern.

Diana took a deep breath to smooth out her irregular heart beat. A trickle of sweat ran from behind one ear and down her neck. She felt numb and disconnected.

A hushed silence fell over the cavern as they entered.

She scanned the room. About a hundred people of varying ages were seated at several rows of wooden plank tables. Her eyes were drawn to a huge fire box and chimney constructed of neatly quarried stone blocks.

The tall man led her to a front table and pulled out a bent-twig chair for her with a flourish. She sat, then realized that the group of white-haired men and women seated at the table facing her were silently staring right at her.

"Please, tell us your story," one of the women said as their eyes met.

After Diana had offered up an abbreviated version of her life on Gaia, the old man seated at the very center of the front table pushed back his chair. He balanced himself carefully with a hand-carved wooden cane, then came around the table and headed directly toward her.

Diana watched as he awkwardly swung his right leg, placing each step carefully. No one stepped up to assist him. She noted how his right shoulder had dropped and rotated to accommodate his awkward, torturous walk. *Old injury,* she thought. *The dragon?*

She waited silently as he came toward her. The only sounds in the cavern were the cracking of the fire, the spitting of the oil lamps, and the rhythmic tap-drag of the old man's walk.

He walked right up to her and propped his cane against the table, then reached out and told hold of Diana's deeply tanned forearms. "We welcome you into our company," he rumbled in a surprisingly powerful voice. "And now let us eat."

He released her arms, retrieved his cane, and headed back to the front table.

Animated conversation filled the cavern the instant the old man settled back into his chair.

Diana was amazed as a salad, steamed grains, a small loaf of fresh baked bread and a rich, spicy stew were placed before her. She turned to the woman seated next to her. "Where do you get your food?"

"We grow it out on the plateau by the upper cave," the woman replied. "Do you like it?"

"It's amazing. But if you have a sunny plateau where you can garden," Diana asked. "Why do you live in this dark cave? Couldn't you build houses out on the plateau?"

From out of the corner of her eye Diana saw the man and woman directly across from her exchange a knowing glance, then turn their attention back to their food.

"Oh," the woman shrugged. "We seldom spend much time on the plateau during the day."

"But, why?" Diana asked.

"The dragon, of course." The woman replied.

"So you spend all of your time in the caves because you're afraid of the dragon?"

The entire table fell silent.

"Well warrior," the older woman sitting on the other side of her snapped, "if you're not afraid of the dragon, why did you run to our cave?"

Diana looked around the table at the faces surrounding her. Few eyes returned her gaze.

The man across from her put his arm around his young son. "There are some things we don't talk about here," he said.

"But what about him?" Diana pointed to the boy. "What chance will he ever have to…to escape from this place."

"Escape?" the man snapped. "What is there to escape? This is the only home he has ever known."

"We are quite comfortable," an older woman added. "And we do go out during the nighttime, and in the early morning before the dragon comes."

Diana felt something she might once have called hope run right out of her. She felt drained – totally empty.

"So, you live here because you're afraid." Her eyes fell to her plate. "And as you noted, I ran here to join you." She pushed her chair back and stood up. "Sorry. I just can't eat."

Diana followed the torches out to the mouth of the cave. The heat of the day still lingered in the evening air.

No one followed her out.

She dropped down hard onto a flat rock and looked out into the evening at what she now knew to be a forbidden land ruled entirely by fear. She had done the very thing she'd been warned to avoid. *Marieji is right*, she thought, *my fear obviously really does own me.*

She stayed there alone until the tall man finally came for her, torch in hand. He gently touched her shoulder.

"It's almost time for the hall torches to go out," he said softly. "Let me show you to a sleeping place.

"Sleep," she shrugged, "does it matter?" She stood and silently followed him.

c3&

CHAPTER TWENTY SEVEN

*In order to conceive of what you truly want
to create, you must first separate what you
want from what you think is possible.*

—Robert Fritz

DIANA BROKE THROUGH her dream – then immediately
became aware of herself both dreaming, and watching herself
dream.

Where am I?

She struggled to free herself from the dizzy vortex of
images and sounds whirling through her mind. She tried
to open her eyes, but the lids were crusted shut. Tried to lift
her right arm to rub her eyes, but discovered that both arms
were restrained at the wrist.

She moved her focus to her ears and identified the whirl
of a machine in the jumble of sounds around her. *A machine?
Here in the caves?*

She pulled in a deep breath, felt her chest expand and

lift, then felt her nostrils flare as she released her breath. An unexpected odor assaulted her – a distinct antiseptic smell. *Hospital. That's it,* she realized. *I'm back in the hospital.*

But am I dreaming or awake?

An internal sense of urgency seeped up from the back of her mind and prodded at her. She took another deep breath and opened her mouth to call for help. Only a faint rasp came out. Her throat was desperately dry and her lips cracked. *Am I making any sound,* she thought. *Or am I just dreaming?*

After several futile attempts to call out, she realized there didn't seem to be anyone to hear her, even if she did manage to make a sound.

The sense of urgency prodded at her again. She suddenly remembered there was some critical reason she had to stay awake – absolutely had to.

To force herself awake she began to sort the images that streamed through her mind – first by color…then by sound, by feeling, and finally by shape.

She saw light coming through what must be a window while peering through a tiny crack in one eyelid. The sensation of cool air slid across her scalp. *Has my head been shaved? Feels like it must have been.*

Steady, throbbing pain pounded through the back of her head.

A brief memory of a fall slid just beyond conscious reach of her mind. She grabbed and caught hold of it. *I fell,* she recalled. *In the street. There was a dragon – something terrible is about to happen to me. What is it?*

She focused again on the details of her hospital

surroundings. Through the tiny crack in her eyelid she followed a tube running from her arm up to an IV bottle.

She reached out further into the environment. What had at first seemed to be a jumble of disconnected voices proved to be two women talking. *Nurses?*

"Go ahead and prep her," the deeper voice said. "She's scheduled for surgery in an hour."

* * * * *

Diana woke in the darkness shivering. She automatically reached out for the hilt of her sword. *Not there.* She grappled wildly for the sword, then jumped to her feet in a panic. The top of her head smacked against the low ceiling of the sleeping cavern.

The blow cracked her mind open into total clarity. She collapsed back down onto the bed.

She knew exactly where she was.

The caves.

"Oh dear self," she moaned. "What have you done?"

೧೩೮೦

CHAPTER TWENTY EIGHT

Where there is no vision, the people perish…

—*The Bible, Proverbs 28:18*

"HELLO, WARRIOR?"

Diana sat upright on the bed.

The tall man who had befriended her extended a torch into the small sleeping cavern. "Want some breakfast? A cup of tea?"

"No. I feel sick all over," Diana replied.

"You've just had a terrible shock," he said. "Why don't we go to the garden – we can get some sun before the dragon comes. Come on, you'll feel better."

She pulled on her clothes, folded the long robe she had worn the night before and placed it on the bed, then stooped to exit through the roughly carved doorway.

He handed her a small green fruit that reminded her

somewhat of a lemon. "Here, this will help settle your stomach."

Diana silently chewed on the sour fruit and walked with him past long rows of flickering torches.

What will happen to me now? she asked herself. *Can I return to the village? Will they take me back in after…after what happened? Probably not.*

She recalled her dream and again remembered she didn't have time to return to the village anyway. *What was it that Marieji told me? "Your time is running out."*

She hesitated when they stepped around a corner into a shaft of bright sunlight. A stairway carved out of a sheer rock wall curved upward toward the source of the light.

"Are you feeling OK?" he asked. "Come on. It's only a short climb."

Diana squinted in the unfamiliar sunlight. *Might as well.* She shrugged her shoulders and set out behind him, indifferent to the large family of pocket bats hanging from the ceiling of a small side cave.

The stairway wound up to an upper crystalline cavern that was almost as large as the lower cavern. The entire mouth of the cave was flooded with bright sunlight.

Diana sucked in a deep breath of the moist, surprisingly sweet air and followed him out onto the sunny plateau.

It was not at all what she had expected.

A sheet of mist rose from a tall waterfall tumbling down the side of the cliff, bathing the entire area in shimmering rainbows. The clear water flowed into a cobalt blue pond surrounded at the far end by tall rushes. Irrigation channels spread out across the garden, distributing the sparkling water to orchards and finely cultivated plots.

He laughed at her surprise. "It's truly a wonderful place, isn't it. Surprised?"

"Amazing."

"Now maybe you can understand why we feel so totally comfortable here."

Incredible, she thought. *Who would believe this could be out here, in the middle of the badlands? Maybe I've been too quick to judge these people.*

"The water is very sweet. Full of natural minerals that feed the garden," he explained. "Come. I'll show you the patch my family keeps."

"Your family?"

"Yes," he smiled. "Although we each came here alone, as you did, we've created our own families."

"Tell me," she looked directly at him, "have you ever thought of leaving? Of going back to the jungle?"

"Of course not."

"But…why?"

"Tell you the truth, there are too many advantages. When I arrived in Gaia I was told I'd surely die if I didn't make it through the dragon's gate immediately. But that was over six years ago. I guess our close presence to the dragon somehow warps time."

"Six years. So…so you're saying that if you stay here–"

"As long as we stay here, we seem to escape the pressure of time."

She stared at him silently. "So maybe I can–"

"You can do the same."

I can stay on Gaia! Diana stood and merged into her surroundings. She was not who she had been. Like raw clay in the hands of a skilled artist, she had been transformed into something totally different. She threw back her head, closed her eyes and breathed in the sweet richness of fruit-laden trees, the hot summer air, the smell of the grass along the path.

She listened to the full song of the world around her, felt its heartbeat move with hers. She had become one with this world. *Truly, I am not who I was.* Gaia was talking to her, talking through her. She could have a place here.

Perhaps I could make peace with myself here. But can I really stay? She waited for her innermost self to answer affirmatively, but instead felt an uncomfortable pressure just beneath her skin.

The answer came.

She felt it invade her being cell by cell. "I can't stay," she said softly.

He stared at her open mouthed. "But there's no way to leave the caves except–"

"Except past the dragon. Right?"

"That's right," he nodded. "But why would you even consider leaving? We have everything you could ever want here – food, safety, companionship, a guarantee of a long life."

Diana walked to the side of the cliff and looked down over the dragon's plateau. A shining object next to a large rock caught her eye.

It was her sword.

He joined her at the edge of the cliff. "Why would you want to leave?"

"Will you spend the rest of your life here?" she asked him, still staring out over the plateau.

"Of course. We all will. Isn't it better to stay here and live, than go down there and just throw your life away for nothing?"

She stood silently and looked long and hard directly into his eyes, then turned again to look out over the plateau where she had faced the dragon.

Perhaps I should stay, she thought. Gaia was in her heart. The very blood moving through her veins was beating to the rhythm of Gaia. She fit in this world. Resonated with it.

She raised her eyes and looked up at the clean azure blue sky. She took a long, deep breath and felt Gaia fill her lungs. *Earth. The pressure, the confusion, the congestion, the anger, the violence, the life-threatening pollution, the uncertainty of even surviving.* "Oh my dear Earth," she sighed. "What have we done to you?"

The man turned and looked at her oddly.

She stooped to pick up a small rock, turned it thoughtfully in her hand, then pressed it to her breast.

He stared at her in confusion.

Diana thoughtfully placed the rock down and looked out over the plateau. "I have to go now," she said quietly. She spun on her heel and strode purposefully toward the stairs leading to the lower cave.

He ran after her. "Go?" He shouted. "Go where?"

"To face the dragon."

"Oh no!" He grabbed her arm. "Don't be stupid!"

"I have to go."

"Why? We've already welcomed you. You can stay–"

"I can't stay. I'm more afraid of staying here out of fear than I am of facing the dragon." She brushed his hand from her arm. "I'm going for the gate."

"There is no gate. They lied to you. No one survives the dragon. I've seen it with my own eyes."

"I have to do it, for myself." She felt his eyes on her back as she started down the stairs.

"Wait," he shouted after her. "Wait."

Diana tightened her belt and walked out of the mouth of the lower cave. She stretched out her arms to receive the warming sun.

The man followed her out two steps, then retreated back into the cave as she stepped out onto the dragon's plateau.

"No," he shouted after her, "don't do it."

She ignored his pleas, strode directly to her sword, and picked it up. She held it up to the sun to inspect the edge, then wiped the dust from the blade with her bandaged hand.

Sharp wailing rose from the mouth of the caves as the people gathered to witness her certain death; but the sound failed to register in Diana's mind.

What had he said? "There is no gate. No one ever survives the dragon."

Diana turned her mind from the man's words. *Just stay present in the now,* she reminded herself. *I need a totally clear mind.*

She sat on a rock to wait for the dragon.

As she waited Diana felt herself begin to waver dangerously, drifting back and forth from the hot plateau, to an extremely cool room – the hospital.

CRESO

CHAPTER TWENTY NINE

The Pleiadians on making an "ascension leap:"
You will simply change the vibrational rate of your
physical being and take your body with you.

— Barbara Marciniak

DIANA SAW A few bright colors through the tiny crack in her eyelid, then a flash of brilliant white – a nurse approaching her bed.

"Prep time," the nurse announced cheerily.

In her dream state Diana felt the nurse run her hand lightly over her shaved skull.

"That'll do," she commented.

Suddenly she clearly remembered what was about to happen.

Her scalp crawled. She had to take action. Now.

Her brain was about to be cut open by a handful of young surgeons.

CHAPTER THIRTY

All living things are interwoven
each with the other. The tie is sacred,
and nothing is alien to anything else.

—*Marcus Aurelius*

THE SUN HAD had just reached its zenith when the shadow of the dragon fell on the plateau.

Diana shook the image of the hospital from her mind and rose, sword in hand, to watch it drop from the sky.

The great winged creature sliced through the air like a knife, braked, then slanted its wings and dropped to the plateau only a few yards from her.

Diana drew in a sharp breath and raised her sword above her head to announce her presence.

The dragon folded huge wings to its sides, then curled its tail around its body – only glancing at the lowly female human who dared present a challenge.

Diana stared in awe as the glistening dragon gracefully rose up to full height and filled its lungs. *It's beautiful,* she thought. *Who would believe this? Looks like it's covered with mirrors.*

The dragon's massive chest swelled, filling the plateau with sparks of rainbow-light as the sunlight reflected off its mirrored scales.

The great beast yawned, then looked directly at her.

Diana watched in a daze as the dragon opened its mouth and the tip of a forked tongue flicked out.

The creature puffed out its huge throat.

The force of the roar swirled a thick cloud of dust around her feet.

Diana's ears pounded as the blood rushed to her brain. She felt fear begin to take hold of her as the large muscles in her legs and back twisted into rock hard spasms. Her stomach knotted into a hard ball.

She steeled herself and took a step forward. "I am Diana," she rasped. "I stand in the face of my fear to–"

The dragon sucked in another deep breath.

A huge ball of fire burst from the dragon's mouth and hurtled through the air directly at her.

She forced herself to hold her ground as the fireball smashed to earth just in front of her, incinerating the sparse ground cover.

Just do it, she screamed inside her own mind. She stepped forward onto the seared earth.

The huge dragon crouched, then sprang into the air.

Diana dropped into the warrior's stance, her sword poised

before her in both hands.

The beast landed but a stone's throw from her.

Once again Diana saw her own image reflected millions of times in the blinding, mirror-like scales. She tore herself from the hypnotic effect, filled her lungs, and roared a warrior's challenge.

The dragon stretched its neck to full length.

Seeing her chance, Diana threw herself at the dragon like a wild animal. She landed between the dragon's two front legs, and jammed her sword into position for a thrust directly into the great beast's heart.

The force of her movement shattered one of the shining mirror-like scales. Time hung suspended as a single drop of crystalline blood formed on the surface of the dragon's shining body…then slowly dropped toward the sun-baked soil.

The single drop of blood was still falling when Diana became lost in the endless rainbow reflections of herself poised to drive her sword directly into the heart of the dragon.

Scenes from her life began to pass before her.

She was five years old in Michigan, walking in the wild birch forest next to the school at the end of the road. The forest floor was covered with lush spring vegetation. Wild violets were in bloom everywhere.

Suddenly she was seven and just had her first view of the Pacific Ocean. She was certain she had looked upon the vastness of the face of God.

Then she was ten and had just discovered that she was an

artist. She had always been so…since early childhood.

What happened to my dreams…to my passion for just being alive? She asked herself.

She watched the glistening drop of blood raise a small crater in the dust, then again looked up and saw herself standing there – suspended in time. The sunlight reflecting off the dragon's scales had covered her with an endless array of shimmering rainbow colors.

With clarity she saw reflections of the tears forming in her own eyes – saw them glisten in the mirror-like scales like finely cut crystals.

What were Marieji's final words. "Beware that you do not thrust the sword into your own heart, just to escape your own fear."

Her warrior's training demanded action. She had to immediately drive her sword into the dragon's heart if she was to survive.

But her heart swelled to a throbbing fullness and spoke quite a different message to her.

She withdrew her sword from the killing position and placed it flat in both hands. "I cannot destroy a being of such great beauty just to escape my own fear and emptiness," she said quietly.

She held the glistening sword up to the dragon, then bent over and laid it at the feet of the great crystalline beast.

The dragon turned one huge eye to look directly at her – directly into her.

For a long moment that stretched out into eternity they stood looking at each other.

Diana saw all of time and space reflected in the dragon's eye – recognized the clear green light shining from it as the same light that had catapulted her through the dragon's gate.

Her life continued to flash before her, frame-by-frame.

Tears burst from her eyes as the great mistakes and sorrows of her life revealed themselves to have been her greatest growth stimuli – each an exquisite and unique moment of truth and discovery.

Diana lifted her open palms to the dragon. "I surrender myself," she said softly.

The people gathered at the edge of the cave shrieked as the great dragon arched its neck and pulled back its head, then fell silent as Diana was engulfed in a roaring cloud of flames.

Diana stood her ground as the flames wrapped around her. Then in the next moment her senses jolted her into a state of ultra sensitivity. *I'm not burning!*

As the roar of the flames subsided, she realized she was in a windy cavern surrounded by almost total darkness. *I must be dead,* she thought. *Wait. The wind. It sounds like...like breathing.*

Her mind went blank with shock. She was inside the dragon.

A commanding voice pierced directly into the center of her mind. "Now shall thy eye be opened," the voice thundered.

Diana spun around as a multi-colored wind swirled around her, then collapsed to her knees and covered her eyes as a brilliant shaft of golden light exploded directly in front of her face.

"Warrior," the voice echoed, "look forth."

Diana cautiously peered through a crack between two fingers, then dropped her hands. Her entire being wavered and began to disassemble. She was looking outward through the eyes of the dragon.

The "skin" of everything surrounding her had become transparent, revealing shifting patterns of pulsating energy where she had formerly seen only solid matter. Even the rocks vibrated in a magical, rhythmic motion. She saw a glistening, endless web of golden light that connected virtually everything. The web extended outward to infinity.

Diana looked down at her own arm and gasped. Her body had merged with the dragon's shimmering body.

She had become one with the dragon.

She sighed, and felt herself become the wind passing over the mountain. Then she became the mountain itself. She felt the solidness, the antiquity of her molecules – the history of mankind passing over her. She felt and became the life force of the many creatures and trees and plants and springs that sprang from her body…from the body of Gaia…from the body of Earth.

Deep within herself the connection between Gaia and Earth – between all beings and planets – was unveiled. The oneness of the solar system, of the entire universe – all parts of the great body of the one great Creative Force.

The group of beings clustered near the mouth of the cave wailing after her caught her attention. Her heart burst open with love and compassion. An overwhelming desire to reach out to them surged and throbbed through her.

Then she felt the dragon's lungs – her lungs – expanding as though to take in the wind itself. Her heart was yet throbbing for the people in the cave when the dragon released its breath in a deafening roar.

She was thrust from the dragon out into the vast darkness of space – became a ball of colored light roaring through the universe like a comet.

Diana surrendered in the darkness into what she intuitively recognized on a deep level to be the music of the spheres – the song of the universe.

＀

CHAPTER THIRTY ONE

The earth is a living planetary being. These observations were made within a scientific context, but go far beyond science to a profound ecological awareness that is ultimately spiritual.

—Fritjof Copra

SHE IMMEDIATELY KNEW the source of the music to be the vibrations coming from the sun, planets, stars, moons, asteroids and yet forming bodies of the solar system – a system of living, breathing planetary beings, of which the Earth was but one.

Her heart yearned for the Earth, reached out to connect with what she truly recognized as her mother. Then her soul swelled to the breaking point as she recognized the blue-green planet beneath her.

She was home.

She felt the depth of her being reach out, flow into, and then embrace the planet on a cellular level.

The North American continent unfolded beneath her.

She felt the atmosphere thicken as she hurtled down toward the surface of the Earth.

Then the lights of LA appeared.

* * * * *

The vision suddenly shattered into millions of mirror-like pieces of a complex puzzle.

Diana struggled to focus, then clearly recognized her surroundings. She was standing in a hospital room in a shimmering pool of light, only an arm's length from her own physical being.

This is no dream, she realized. *I'm really here.*

Two orderlies had lifted her body from the hospital bed and placed her on the gurney about to transport her to the operating room.

Diana immediately realized that there were only weak signs of life in the still body – her body.

She remembered one of Marieji's warnings. *"If you do return successfully through the gate, you will face yet another great moment of truth. You must focus solidly enough in your body to overcome the hold of the coma. It won't be easy."*

Diana looked at the still body and sighed at the memory of the strength she had built on Gaia. *Gaia.* Her heart ached.

She heard Marieji's voice in her mind. *"Choose, Diana."*

She tested her connection to the still body. It was still alive, but the brain was almost totally asleep. *What if I can't break through,* she thought. *What if I get stuck in that coma?*

Can't allow my fear to own me, she reminded herself. She

set the resolve of her intention, took a deep breath, then relaxed and allowed her full consciousness to flow into the still body.

* * * * *

Diana felt herself lying on the gurney. She tried to move her arms and legs, but couldn't quite connect her intentions with the long-abandoned physical self.

She heard the sound of footsteps and peered out through the tiny crack in the slightly opened eyelid. A nurse was approaching the gurney.

"OK guys, take her to Op Three," the nurse said.

No. Wait! Diana screamed silently.

One of the orderlies jerked the end of the gurney.

I've got to do something.

"Wait a second, guys." The nurse bent over to tighten the strap around Diana's waist.

Diana saw what could be her last chance to save herself from the surgeons. *Intent,* she commanded herself. "Wa…ter," she rasped.

"Oh my God," the nurse exclaimed. "I think she just tried to speak. Wait," she shouted at the orderlies. Diana heard the woman rush out of the room.

Please come back, Diana thought desperately. *Please.*

The flash of white returned.

Diana heard the scrape of metal against metal as the nurse slid a pan of warm water onto a metal tray near the gurney.

"Wa…ter," she rasped.

The nurse placed the long spout of a plastic bottle in her

mouth and squeezed out a few drops.

Diana sighed involuntarily as warm water suddenly bathed her eyelids. She tried to open her lids but the nurse placed her fingers lightly over her eyes.

"Keep your eyes closed for a moment. Let's clean them up a little. Go get Dr. Brennan," she shouted at one of the orderlies.

Wild streams of tears gushed down Diana's cheeks as she opened her eyes in the bright hospital room.

CHAPTER THIRTY TWO

There are no coincidences in the universe.

—*Neale Donald Walsch*

"EVERYTHING LOOKS SO different," Diana commented to herself as she walked out her back door.

Ever since she had been released from the hospital two days ago, it had seemed as though the edges of everything were somehow sharper. Colors seemed brighter. Sounds more intense. Smells more pungent.

Still, she had been constantly hounded by a disturbing feeling that there was something she needed to remember. It was something just out of reach of her conscious mind, but she know it was of great importance.

As she settled onto a weathered chair by the back door, her eyes were drawn to a brilliant red primrose that had suddenly bloomed by the back of the house.

"Life is such a miracle," she sighed. "Last week nothing

but dried weeds – and now a beautiful little flower. Bet there was a flower garden there once." She got up, stooped down next to the primrose, and began to clear away weeds from around the little flower.

An hour later she had uncovered several primroses and geraniums that still had life in them. She searched the garage, found an old hose, and dragged it out to water the flowers.

A Siamese cat suddenly slid out of the bushes and stood staring at her.

"So who are you?" Diana looked at the obviously hungry feline, her ribs showing beneath a ragged coat. "Come here, girl," she coaxed. "You look hungry." She extended her open hand to the cat.

The instant her fingertips touched the cat's head, an odd sensation of familiarity slid through Diana's mind. The cat pushed its head against her hand.

"Do I know you?" she asked the cat. "Seems like maybe I do, somehow."

"Mee…ee…ow." The Siamese stared directly into Diana's eyes.

Diana laughed as an unexpected warm glow of joy rushed into her chest. "Looking for a new home?" She went into the kitchen and returned with a bowl of tuna.

The cat had waited by the back door.

"OK. Consider yourself adopted."

The cat attacked the food.

"Do make yourself at home," Diana laughed. "You know, little friend," she commented as she watched the cat devour the tuna. "I feel like something truly wonderful is coming to life inside me. I'm not sure what to call it. A mystery maybe – a deep longing for something that...that has real truth and meaning."

"Mee...eep," the cat commented between bites.

"I feel this fullness here in my heart for the Earth, and a total lack of worry about my life. Does that sound strange?"

"Mee...eep."

Diana noticed a stunted lemon tree with a few shriveled lemons still hanging from it by the back fence. She left the cat to its food and dragged the hose over to the tree, washed it down, then placed the hose on the ground to soak the roots.

Suddenly she became aware that someone was watching her. She turned, and saw the old woman who lived in the next door cabin standing where two boards were missing in the side fence.

"It's good to care for that brave little tree," the woman nodded solemnly.

Diana stared at the woman in silence for a moment before she realized who she was. It was Rosa, the woman her neighbor's teenage daughter called "the crazy old wise woman."

"We may soon need the seeds of such trees," the old woman smiled. "Bring one of those dried up lemons and I'll show you how to start a whole grove from the seeds. And bring that warrior cat with you."

A red light exploded directly in front of Diana's eyes at the woman's words. "Warrior?" She staggered as a current of electricity roared up her spine and into her head.

A whirlwind of memories flooded through her mind and out again – just beyond conscious recognition.

"Are you alright?" The woman bent over to pet the cat, who had come directly to her.

"Yes, but I just–" Diana stuttered.

"OK, I'll go. I see you prefer to be alone." The old woman turned and started to walk back toward her cabin.

"No. Please, wait!" Diana called to the old woman. She picked one of the dried lemons, then squeezed through the hole in the fence.

The woman turned and silently waited for her.

Diana felt time twist back on itself as she stopped directly in front of the woman and their eyes met. Flickering, barely recognizable, images of a jungle, a dragon, a great moment of truth raced through her mind.

The old woman returned her gaze, smiled, then reached out and lightly touched Diana on the shoulder.

The touch grounded her and the memories clarified. Diana staggered, and looked back at the woman. For a brief moment time and space vanished into oneness.

"Come, let's have a cup of tea and talk," the woman said softly. "I can see a light burning within that begs for fuel."

About the Author

Although born in Michigan, author Jill Ammon-Wexler considers herself a native California mountain woman. Her passions include personal transformation, writing and speaking, gardening, metaphysics, good conversation, physical fitness, downhill skiing, road cycling, and generally being in nature. As a Doctor of Psychology, she was a pioneer in the use of state-of-the-art brainwave training and color-encoded therapy for personal growth and enhanced performance training. She currently lives in a Northern California redwood forest.

Clear Vision Press

Post Office Box 608
Capitola, California 95010-0608
USA
Clearvis@cruzio.com